DEATH WALTZ

Sharon K. Robinson

Fulton Books, Inc.
Meadville, PA

Published by Fulton Books 2020

ISBN 978-1-64952-476-8 (paperback)
ISBN 978-1-64952-477-5 (digital)

Printed in the United States of America

ACKNOWLEDGMENTS

I want to thank my beautiful daughter, Aimee Phillips, whom the dynamic personality of Charlee is based upon. She inspired me with many ideas for the story. Also, for my son, David Price, for his creative input. I'd like to include my lively grandchildren—Kiera, Kohner, Kameron, and Akaysha. Thank you to my sister, Heidi, whose support was motivational. Lastly, in memory of my lovely mother, Helen Price, and my aunt, Carlene Pajong. Plus, thank you to all my family and friends who have to listen to me repeatedly tell them, "Guess what? I have a story…"

PROLOGUE

Rogue River, Oregon, July 4, 1950

The patchy road moved quickly beneath their powder-blue Buick convertible as it raced along West Evans Creek Road. The road was lined with tall evergreen trees, and the night was dark with just a sliver of the moon. Bouncing along potholes in the road, Charles swerved to avoid the nearby ditches. "Damn!" Charles swore as a deer leaped across the roadway. Marilyn, his wife, giggled and raised her glass half-filled with champagne and took a long gulp. The summer air was warm with a gentle breeze and lifted her long blond hair gently around her beautiful face.

"Charles! You do know I love you so, right? Just because that silly man was paying attention to me at the party...it didn't mean a thing!" Her face tilted up to him, her eyes sparkling with mischief. Charles was such an attractive man—tall, dark, striking, but sometimes so stodgy about following rules. She had always thought he was her Clark Gable, and she was his Carole Lombard. "You are driving a little crazy fast on this road, although you do drive like one of those irresistible race drivers!" She laughed breathlessly. Charles looked at her with frustration and adoration.

Marilyn looked up, startled, as a bright light flashed into her blue eyes. "Oh my God, Charles, watch out!"

Charles, on the wrong side of the road, was headed straight into an oncoming car. He grabbed the wheel, yanked it viciously to the right, and drove off the side of the road into a small ditch, landing with a jolt. The other car, a large gray Ford sedan, swerved with its brakes screeching, went off the road, and struck a tree head-on with a gut-clenching sound of glass breaking, screaming, and then a deadly silence.

The world had seemed to stop. Dust rose in the air. They were alive! Marilyn pushed open the door and made it to the side of the road where she convulsively threw up all the champagne she had drunk and all those lovely gourmet treats. Charles stumbled drunkenly over to the other car. The old Ford was tilted slightly upward, lodged in the large oak tree with smoke pouring out over the hood. The front of the car was crumpled, and the windshield broken. It was quiet. Charles peered inside the window. There was a young couple sitting slouched over in the front seat, seemingly unconscious with blood dripping from their faces. The woman's brown eyes stared out vacantly, with the vapid look of a doll. The man's head was turned in an awkward, impossible angle. Charles, with difficulty, yanked open the bent door. *Oh my God! They are so young!* His cloudy mind was clearing up to the enormity of the situation. He awkwardly reached in and felt for their pulses—stillness. They were dead. Then a thin wail filled the air. On the back seat was an overturned baby-carrier bassinet. The baby, trapped underneath, screamed louder and louder. Charles lifted the bassinet out of the way and stared in shock at the terrified baby.

"Oh Charles! A baby!" Marilyn stumbled over to the car. She leaned into the back seat. "And she's a girl. Look at the pink blanket and her sweet little bonnet!" She reached in to pat her lovingly. "It's okay, darling. Mama is here!" Marilyn's eyes held a faraway look. "Charles, we found her! Isn't she lovely?"

Charles looked into his wife's mad eyes. The moonlight lit up her face in an eerie glow. "Yes, sweetheart! Truly lovely!" Charles reached in and swept up the baby in the bassinet, looking furtively over his shoulder. "Anything for you, my darling."

CHAPTER 1

Rogue River, Oregon, 1978

It was a blustery fall day; and leaves swirled down the street, lazily falling from the large orange and golden trees. The air was crisp, and the scent of newly awakened fireplaces touched the air.

Fall was always so lovely and colorful in Southern Oregon with the change of season. There was a sense of renewed hope and of letting go of the past—a time for change.

Charlee looked out the French windowpanes of her front door and observed the weather. "Well, Chewy, should we take a walk and acquaint ourselves with the neighborhood? I feel pretty certain we'll get their attention, ya think?" she said with a derisive smile. Her right eyebrow lifted high with humor. Her dark-brown eyes sparkled mischievously.

Chewy's large head tilted. His ears lifted, with his tail wagging, and he barked softly in agreement. Chewy was a large male Saint Bernard and was about two years old. He took up a lot of space in the small two-bedroom house that Charlee had recently bought in Rogue River, Oregon. His soft, soulful brown eyes gazed longingly at the leash hanging near the front door.

"Okay, Chewy!" Charlee threw her head back and laughed. "You are so obvious! Let's go!" She clicked the leash onto Chewy's collar and smiled at Chewy affectionately. She had named him after Chewy, the large man-beast on her favorite movie, *Star Wars*, which had come out the year before, and she had waited in a line to the theater that wrapped around the block. She was an avid fan of *Star Wars*,

Sharon K. Robinson

and it reflected in some of her artwork that she proudly displayed on the walls. Her collectibles were still lying in unpacked boxes.

As she opened the front door, a chilly burst of wind struck her face and lifted her hip-length curly auburn hair. Her hair was thick and beautiful, and she was often complimented on it. "Whew, a little chilly there! Well, come on. Let's check this ole town out!"

Chewy barked happily and lunged forward, nearly lifting five-foot-two Charlee off her feet. She laughed with delight at the power and strength of her dog, thinking to herself, *Maybe I should buy a saddle or a wagon that he could drag me in for a ride?*

CHAPTER 2

She snapped off her living-room light and stepped out onto Oak Street in front of her house. Her little blue one-story, two-bedroom house was built in 1910 and was directly across from the elementary school which was over one hundred years old. The school sat adjacent to the Woodville Museum, a beautiful white Victorian-style building with a gazebo. In the summer time, bands would play in the gazebo during the town's annual event of Rooster Crow, which was a yearly celebration with a parade, booths selling a little bit of "this and that," carnival food, and a competition of locals' roosters of which who could crow the longest and the loudest. It was a little silly, but everybody loved it. And it was an ongoing event that the town looked forward to yearly. In the backyard of the museum was a one-room brick jailhouse consisting of two small cells. *I bet that little jail house, if it could talk, would have a lot of interesting stories*, Charlee mused to herself. *Maybe ghost stories?* Her hair lifted with a breeze, and she felt a little chill.

The little town of Rogue River had an interesting past with marauding Indians, a tough one-legged frontier sheriff at the turn of the century, the KKK, gamblers, floods, and still boasted a population of two thousand. It had claimed that population for decades.

Chewy pulled her happily with enthusiasm toward Main Street. The little town was quaint and reminded her of the old TV series *Mayberry.* There was a little barbershop with the striped bar outside, a few diners, two gas stations, and the Homestead Bar and Restaurant. On the center of Depot and Main Street was a sculpture of a rooster nestled in a tree. Charlee smiled. *This town is really into roosters. How funny!*

Across from the corner of the proud rooster was an antique store named Rambling Rose. Peggy, the feisty little owner, had been there for years. She was an enthusiastic buyer of antiquities. Whenever she acquired a treasured antique, she would laugh and swear with gusto. She loved to shock people with her colorful vocabulary. Peggy stood at least five feet tall, had short dark hair, had a raucous laugh, and swore like a sailor. Everybody loved her!

Charlee loved antiques and was drawn to the store like a child to a candy counter. She peered through the large window, cupping her eyes with her hands. *Wow! The place is filled with antiques!* Her eyes were drawn to an antique typewriter that was placed atop an old secretary desk. *Wow! That must be at least one hundred years old.* Charlee had a passion for writing. She had left her real-estate career in Lake Arrowhead, California, to move to Oregon to pursue her writing. She had a degree in journalism but had gotten sidetracked into the real-estate world to make money, which she had, but she wasn't happy or fulfilled. She had done very well for being twenty-eight years old, but she knew there was more to life than just a healthy bank account.

She wrapped Chewy's leash around the antique bench that sat outside the store. "Now, stay here and behave Chewy! No running down the street dragging that bench behind you, okay?"

Chewy looked at her sadly with large droopy brown eyes and a lolling tongue. Charlee pushed open the door, which acknowledged her presence with jangling Santa bells that were tied to it.

Peggy greeted her with a smile. "Is that your horse you parked outside? He's gonna scare the hell out of any potential customers!" Peggy laughed and said, "Aw, never mind, come on in! Are you new to the area or visiting?"

Peggy stood there with one hand on her skinny denim-clad hip. She wore cowboy boots and a long tunic sweater. "Hey, you want some coffee?"

Charlee smiled, pushed her hair back, and walked farther into the store. Her eyes took in the numerous antiques which were crowded on the walls, floors, shelves, and any available surface. "Your old typewriter caught my eye." She walked over to the typewriter and gingerly touched it with her fingertips. Quickly she drew back her hand, feeling a slight electrical shock. Gasping slightly, she said, "It looks like it's in pretty good condition. Does it work?" she asked hopefully.

"Yeah, it works. It still even has a ribbon in it," Peggy stated matter-of-factly, hoping for a sale. The typewriter was a dust collector and had sat there for a long time, and frankly, she thought it a little ugly and creepy.

There was a piece of paper in the typewriter, and Charlee struck the *T* key several times, and a bold *T* clacked onto the paper.

"How much?"

"Seventy-five dollars." She smiled curiously at Charlee and asked, "Ya really want it? I would've taken you as a fancy electric-typewriter gal—not that I'm trying to talk you out of it."

"Oh, I love my Olympia typewriter too, but I love collecting antiques. And besides, I'm a writer," Charlee said happily, excited with her discovery of the typewriter. "I'll take it!"

"You won't be taking it anywhere right now."

Charlee's head came up. "Why not?"

"It's too heavy! You're walking. You couldn't possibly carry that thing."

Charlee attempted to lift the typewriter. "Wow! You're right! This must weigh at least forty pounds!" She looked at the typewriter in amazement. "Can I pay for it now and pick it up tomorrow?"

"You bet! I'm not gonna refuse that offer!" Peggy walked over to her antique cash register as Charlee dug into her pocket for her credit card. She handed her card over with a huge smile, dimples flashing.

CHAPTER 3

After Charlee left the antique store, she slowly walked up the street, exploring more of the town. She passed the library, a few restaurants, Sentry's grocery store; and at the end of Main Street, she turned left onto Wards Creek Road to check out Woodville Cemetery. *Cemeteries are so interesting*, she thought. *I love reading the gravestones— so much history and so many stories.* She walked around the graveyard quietly. Some of the markers were over a hundred years old.

The place was deserted and quiet. It was a rather forlorn little cemetery—a mixture of the old with the new. Some graves were adorned with flowers and little gifts. Some were overgrown and covered with weeds. Looking sadly at the weeds, she thought, *The buried have been long forgotten.*

Her attention was drawn to a small tombstone with a statue of a baby angel perched on top. The angel's face was cracked, and one of its wings had a large chip in it. *Anna Marie.* The date of birth was 1920, and the death at 1921. She leaned in to read the inscription, which was a little difficult as some of the words had worn down with time. "Our little angel, our lives will never be the same." *Aw…how sad is that!* she thought to herself.

There was a sudden gust of wind, and orange and brown leaves swirled around her feet and then lifted up into the gray sky. A large dark cloud passed over the sun. She shivered, feeling a little pensive and, suddenly, sad. Chewy seemed to sense her mood and wagged his tail apprehensively. "Damn, Chewy, let's get out of here before I start crying for God knows what—or who!" As they walked out of the cemetery, Charlee looked back over her shoulder, with a troubled look on her face, and wiped away a solitary tear.

CHAPTER 4

After a brisk walk home, Charlee unlocked the front door; and Chewy dashed inside toward his water bowl, which he began to slurp from noisily. Puzzled, Charlee looked around the lit room. *That's funny. I distinctly remember turning off the light when we left. Damn, I hope there aren't any electrical issues here, and it is so freaking cold in here.* She turned the temperature gauge up a notch. Wrapping her sweater tightly around her, she thought, *Maybe I should have a hot toddy instead of a beer?*

CHAPTER 5

Charlee lugged the heavy typewriter out to her Jeep parked outside the antique store. With a mighty heave, she hoisted it onto the passenger front seat. "I can't believe how heavy this thing is," she said in gasps to Peggy, who was standing behind her, holding the door.

"Ha, I know, right? Ya can't tell by looking at it. Well, I hope you enjoy it and you'll come back and visit my store again. Hell! Just come in for a cup of coffee if you like," Peggy said with a friendly smile. "Bye now!"

She parked in front of her house, ran up her steps, and unlocked the door, bracing it open. Getting a firm grasp on the typewriter, she lugged it up the stairs into her house and placed it with a loud clunk on the little antique desk in her second bedroom. "Whew! Done," she said proudly.

She stepped back in admiration. The sheer gauze curtain on the window behind the desk added a soft hue. She placed her small antique dictionary near the typewriter and a small old gooseneck lamp. *Perfect! Very cool! I love the ambience of this house*, she mused to herself, *the heavy wood paneling, hardwood floors, and the incredibly old nonfunctioning fireplace. The bathroom is tiny, but at least it had a bathtub you could lean back on comfortably. Ha! My parents would hate it and think it very unfashionable and rustic.*

Her parents were always on top of the latest trends and fashions and were very unhappy with her move to Oregon. She couldn't explain her inexplicable draw to move to Rogue River and this little outdated, quaint cabin. Her mother would call it a *hovel*, emphasizing the word with a French accent. She sighed. *Of all places...*

But it was her choice. She smiled happily to herself and went out to the kitchen to start her dinner of pork stir-fry. She popped the top off a Corona and placed the pork into the sizzling pan. Yep, she loved this meal, and she was a damn good cook.

Wrapping her arms around herself tightly, she shivered. *Why in the world is it so cold in here?* She walked over and tapped the thermometer. *Well, damn, it says it's seventy-three degrees in here.* She looked around feeling puzzled. Chewy sat quietly staring at her, his tail wagging slowly on the floor. Suddenly, Chewy emitted a low rumbling growl. There was a clacking sound coming from the second bedroom, her "office" she now called it. *Oh my God! Is somebody here? Did they open the window and that's why it's so cold?* Thoughts flashed through her mind. She reached for a heavy iron skillet off the stove and began to tiptoe to the office. Chewy walked silently besides her, seeming to understand the necessity for stealth. She slowly pushed open the door, with the pan held high over her head, and walked into the room. There was nobody there, and the window was shut. It was freezing! Her breath created steam in the air. The hair on the back of her neck rose. What the hell was going on? Chewy growled again, his fur bristling. She had never seen him do that before. She walked over to test the window, making sure it was locked. She looked down at the typewriter. There was a line of typing in bold capital letters—I HAVE THE STORY!

With a sharp intake of breath, Charlee whispered aloud, "What?" The curtain suddenly billowed out around the desk wildly, slapping against her face; and she heard a breathy whisper nearby, close to her ear, "I have the story!"

Charlee let out a small shriek, and Chewy began barking loudly and ferociously facing—seemingly—nothing.

CHAPTER 6

With a loud bang, Charlee slammed the bedroom door behind her, nearly catching Chewy's tail in the jamb. Her heart was pounding, and she was shaking deeply and uncontrollably. *What in the world just happened? That was crazy!* She heard the pork sizzling on the stove and went to it, stirring automatically. She steadied herself.

Chewy sat next to her on the floor where she had collapsed near the stove. His head tilted to one side; and his ears lifted, listening for a sound. She could sense his air of extreme alertness. She had no doubts that Chewy would protect her with his life if need be. He was such a good dog and friend.

The room began to warm up, and Charlee popped open another beer. *How in the world am I going to sleep tonight? What happened in there? The print,* I HAVE THE STORY, *and that whisper. It was so clearly spoken—so damn eerie. I couldn't have imagined it, but how could it be?* She had never really thought about ghosts much since being a young girl at slumber parties, where they would try to scare and shock each other with horrifying stories. Charlee was a little proud to admit she always told the scariest stories. But this really just happened. Should she tell anyone? She was new here, and if she shared that news, they would think she was as crazy as an outhouse mouse.

Charlee went through all the normal motions—putting on her warm flannel pajamas, brushing her teeth, washing her face—and began to tiptoe into her bedroom. She paused outside her office with her ear to the door. *Well, all's quiet in this side of the haunted house,* she mused. Chewy walked silently behind her. Once inside her room, she pulled back the covers, climbed in, and looked at Chewy sitting on the floor with his gaze intently upon her. "Oh, you know it, Chewy! You're sleeping with me tonight!"

Chewy gave a snort of approval and bounced on top of the bed beside her. They both snuggled into each other, and Charlee hoped it would be a restful night without any more strange disturbances.

Chapter 7

Charlee awoke the next morning with a start, pulling herself out of a vague and disturbing dream. *What was it?* The remnants of the dream were rapidly dissipating. *Falling leaves and a baby crying? Didn't make sense.* Chewy looked at her with sleep-glazed eyes. *Boy, that dog could sleep!* He could sleep in longer than her any day of the week.

With determination, she pulled on her sweats, tennis shoes, and a jacket and ventured outside into the frosty morning. Walking around the side of the house, she went under the window to the office. She looked closely around the area, searching for footprints and looking for a possible, logical explanation for the seemingly supernatural experience. The ground was wet and soft, devoid of a single footprint of any kind. There was no sign of disturbance around the window frame. *Well, what the hell happened here?* she thought.

She walked slowly back into the house and forced herself to reenter her office. Chewy reluctantly followed her into the room. Everything was quiet, so very quiet, still, and cold. There was a feeling of tense expectation in the air. *Am I imagining this?* she wondered. Almost stealthily, she walked over to the typewriter, and there just as it was last night—the paper with the typed words in bold capital letters: I HAVE THE STORY! She swung her head around, having a feeling that somebody was in the room watching her. Chewy seemed to sense it too. His ears were laid back, his hair bristling and a very low growl emanating from his jowls. *Holy crap, now what?* It was all that came to mind.

CHAPTER 8

The following evening, carrying a cup of hot chocolate with whipped cream, Charlee sat down at her kitchen table with her electric typewriter. She just couldn't bring herself to try and work in her office right now. She tried to push down any thoughts of all that scary crap. She needed to get back into the practice of writing, and the only way to do that was to write. *So here I am*, she thought wryly to herself. She decided to start writing her first impressions of her move to Rogue River—the town, the swiftly moving river, and the friendly people.

She left out the scary stuff even though she knew that was really the interesting stuff that people loved to read about. But she didn't want to be known as some sort of eccentric right off the bat. She sincerely wanted to stay in Rogue River and to fit in with the locals. She loved the small-town atmosphere, like living in Lake Arrowhead. *What a great place to grow up!* Nostalgically remembering the warm lazy afternoons of hanging out in the Lake Arrowhead village with her friends, she smiled. It was a time of no worries, laughter, innocent flirtations, and no thoughts of tomorrow. *Seize the day!* came to her mind. Things had certainly changed since becoming an adult. *Yuck*, she thought ruefully. *What was I thinking?*

Her childhood had been pretty pampered. She knew her parents loved her, but they always seemed to live in their own little bubble. *I always felt a little like a bystander, or maybe even a guest*, Charlee wondered. Her father had always seemed so sad and distracted, but he nearly always complied with her requests. He was really adept in the real-estate world and taught her everything to help her become successful in the field. Her mother was beautiful, moody, and prone to long migraine headaches, where she would stay days in her darkened room. *I felt so lonely sometimes*, Charlee thought sadly. There were no brothers or sisters. Thank God she had been blessed with so many friends. They had kept her going and laughing. All those days on the lake skiing, hiding wine bottles lowered on ropes beneath the boat, and laughing till they were hoarse—those lovely golden days.

CHAPTER 9

Okay, okay! I'm rabbit-trailing, an expression she used when she was getting off track. She positioned herself over the keys again and began happily typing. Suddenly the lights flickered, and then the power went off. She was sitting in the dark. She sat there for a moment, contemplating what she was going to do next. She strained her eyes in the darkness, knowing there was a candle somewhere. *Maybe on the mantel of the fireplace?* Carefully she walked over, fumbling, and found the candle and lit it. Chewy's face, now illuminated, looked up at her quizzically.

The air suddenly was colder. Steam rose upon her breath. *Uh-oh*, she thought. Chewy's growl was low and soft. The hair on the back of her neck rose. The door to her office opened and slammed shut and then opened and slammed shut again and again and again. The typing paper Charlee had on the table beside her typewriter rose in the air, swirling furiously in a circle above her head. The paper was swirling so quickly. She ducked her head and put her hands in front of her face, protecting herself from numerous paper cuts.

Charlee screamed and sat down on the floor, her arms above her head protecting herself. A low voice rising in intensity screamed out, "I HAVE THE STORY! I HAVE THE STORY!" The voice was intense, and she could not tell if it was male or female. It was loud and rang in her ears and mind. It was deafening. This was crazy—too much! Charlee maintained her crouch. Chewy ran over to her and, using his body as a shield, protected her from the crazy whirling papers—a paper tornado. And then it stopped. The voice, the noise—it seemed to be sucked out of the room like a vacuum. The papers drifted to the floor. It was over. The air warmed. The fearful intensity was gone.

It was like the door shutting out a storm. Charlee shook uncontrollably, and Chewy gave her big sloppy kisses all over the back of her head. She cried. *What in the world am I doing here? Am I nuts? My family is far away, and I'm in this little downtrodden house with no job, no man in my life, no kids, nothing.* She put her head back and let out a wail of an unhappy woman in a strange town with no support.

CHAPTER 10

Days passed and no writing. Charlee would stare at that blank page on her Olympia typewriter every morning over her cup of coffee. She remembered Hemingway had once said something about nothing being more terrifying than a blank page. She understood that now. It had taken on a whole new meaning to her.

Every day she and Chewy would go for long walks along the river, through the town, and explore the local parks—Fleming, Coyote Evans, and Palmerton. They were all so beautiful even though most of the fall leaves had now fallen, and winter was on the way.

It was getting close to Thanksgiving, and the air was crisp. Charlee threw a stick to Chewy again for what seemed to be the hundredth time, and he happily chased after it again. He loved the parks! Sighing, she placed her thermos of coffee on the scruffy picnic table and climbed up and laid down on it, staring up into that vast gray sky. The rushing and swollen Rogue River was gray too, matching the sky above. Large dark cumulus clouds were gathering, and she knew there would be rain again soon. Rain had lost its charm. There was just too much of it. The large trees above her were barren of leaves—naked shivering trees.

She closed her weary eyes. She hadn't been sleeping very well since these crazy occurrences at her house. *It's so weird,* she thought. *I want to write, but I'm afraid to. Something about the typewriter...but that's just so crazy. I hope I haven't made a huge mistake moving here.* She heard a rumble of thunder and looked up and saw a flash in the sky. A few raindrops misted her face. A wave of homesickness for Lake Arrowhead came over her, and she held back her tears tightly.

"Whoa! What's that pinched-up face for? Are you in pain?" a concerned but teasing voice asked.

"What!" Charlee sat up with a start, knocking her thermos over. Chewy came galloping over to her side, barking softly at the stranger. A tall man stood there looking at Charlee inquisitively.

"I'm sorry. Didn't mean to scare you or Tonto here. Boy, is he huge!"

The first thing Charlee noticed was his badge—a cop. And then she expected some kind of trouble. But then she looked into his smiling blue eyes and the laugh that he was trying to hold back. He had dark curly hair, a little long for being a cop she noticed. He seemed tall, but everyone seemed tall to her because she was short. She sat up a little straighter, told Chewy to hush, and then scowled, which made this cop smile wider.

"Oh, I'm sorry. You just caught me by surprise. Sneak up on everyone like that?" Charlee said, smiling reluctantly, and her one eyebrow lifted questioningly.

"Only when I see women sleeping on picnic tables out in the rain," he said with a laugh. "Hi! I'm Deputy Corbin O'Malley. I haven't seen you around before. Visiting? Or have you moved to the area?" He stretched out his hand and shook her hand firmly.

"Yes, I recently moved here about a month ago, and I wasn't sleeping—just resting after playing with Chewy for what seems like hours. He never gets tired of chasing a stick." Chewy wagged his tail enthusiastically and leaned in toward the deputy, allowing him to pat his head.

"He really is a big boy! Chewy? Chewbacca from *Star Wars*?"

She nodded.

"I love that movie! I think it's a perfect name for him," he said, smiling down at Chewy. "Hey, I wouldn't be a thorough cop if I didn't ask you your name!" His friendly smile lit up his face, and Charlee couldn't help noticing he had smiling Irish eyes.

"I'm Charlee Wilkes," she said with a smile, her dimples flashing. She pulled the hood of her jacket over her head. "Well, I guess it really is starting to rain. We should start heading back. Nice meeting you! Come on, Chewy. Let's go!" She clamped the leash onto Chewy's collar and stood up.

"Very nice meeting you too, Charlee! Hope to see you around." He tipped his head at her and smiled. *She sure is pretty*, he thought. *Something is troubling her, or maybe she's sad.*

She had looked like she was about to cry when he had spotted her lying on the picnic table. He watched her departing figure wistfully. *I hope I see her again*, he thought to himself.

As she walked as gracefully as she could up the hill to the parking lot, she could feel his eyes on her. She couldn't resist it. Looking over her shoulder, she saw him standing there watching her. Of course, he noticed she saw him, and he raised his hand to her, waving goodbye.

Charlee smiled to herself. *Damn, he was cute!*

Rounding the corner to her house, she picked up her pace. All the lights were on in her house, and she was positive she had turned them off when she left.

"Damn, Chewy! Let's run!" They sprinted to her house. Her neighbor was standing out front, looking annoyed. Music was blasting from her house at top volume. "What the hell?" Charlee whispered under her breath.

"You shouldn't have your music on so loud! We can hear it from our house, and frankly, it's annoying," her neighbor Wilamena whined, shaking with anger. Her gray flinty eyes, surrounded by crow's-feet, glared at Charlee. Her hair was tightly pulled up into a gray knot on top of her head; and the wind had blown the bun slightly askew, giving her a rather comical Leaning Tower of Pisa look.

"I didn't leave the music on! And why don't you mind your own business?" she snapped. Charlee ran up her stairs with Chewy following close behind her. She threw open the door and ran straight to the stereo. The song that was reverberating at the highest volume was the song "You Are My Sunshine." The incongruity of the sweet, innocent song to the frightening situation gave her chills. She flipped the power off. Bewildered, she looked around the house. Every light and mechanical appliance was on. The blender whirred in the background. She walked around the house, unplugging the blender, the toaster, coffeepot, her hair dryer in the bathroom, and flipping every light switch off. "What the hell," she thought aloud, standing in the middle of her living room in the growing darkness.

Wilamena stood outside on the sidewalk, mouth gaping open, "Well, what a rude young woman!" She turned on her heel and marched angrily back to her house, slamming her door behind her.

CHAPTER 11

After another restless night of little sleep, Charlee stumbled into the kitchen, made a pot of coffee, poured a bowl of Lucky Charms cereal, and sat wearily down at her kitchen table. She stirred her cereal around, finally forcing herself to a spoonful. Normally, she loved eating kids' cereals, but this morning, she just felt completely exhausted. Pouring herself a large cup of coffee, she felt her mind slowly becoming more alert with every sip.

I need to stop being afraid of every shadow and start finding out what is going on around here, she thought with a dawning determination. *Yep, and I know just where to start!*

Quickly, she got dressed in her blue jeans and pulled a black hooded sweatshirt over her head. Pulling her hair into a ponytail, she looked at her reflection in the bathroom mirror. *Wow! I look so pale, and I have dark shadows under my eyes.* Her eyes looked haunted and stared back sadly at herself. She pinched her cheeks, and a little color came back into her face.

Snapping the leash onto Chewy, she stepped out into the brisk air. "Let's go, Chewy, and see if we can get some answers!"

They walked at a fast pace all the way to Peggy's antique store. Charlee tied up Chewy again at the antique bench outside the store. Chewy looked forlornly at her and ducked his head.

"Oh, you'll be okay! Don't be a baby, Chewy," she chastised him.

He hung his head lower, looking a little embarrassed. *He sure is expressive.* She smiled. Before she had Chewy, she never would have thought that dogs could show embarrassment.

The Santa bells jangled loudly behind her as she entered the store. "Well, hey there, Charlee!" Peggy greeted her with a wide smile. "I was hoping you'd come back! How are…?" Her voice trailed off. "What's wrong, Charlee? It's written all over your face, and you look exhausted. Plus, you look like you've lost weight, and as tiny as you are, that's not good. You look like hell," Peggy said with concern in her voice.

Charlee looked so tired and thin and had a stretched, tight look about her like she was very stressed out. *Could she be homesick? I wonder what's going on.* She pulled her hands out of her overall pockets, arms outstretched, and gave Charlee a big motherly hug. "I just made a pot of coffee. And I have chocolate doughnuts, and I'll tell you that chocolate can fix just about anything!" She laughed deeply.

Charlee sat down on the offered chair, biting her lip. Why was it when someone was so genuinely nice to her, she felt like bawling her eyes out? She smiled up at Peggy with tears welling up in her eyes. "I love chocolate doughnuts," she said tremulously.

"Of course you do," Peggy said triumphantly. Pouring them both coffee and laying out the doughnuts, Peggy said, "Okay, spill it! I know you don't know me all that well, but whatever you tell me goes no further. And I think right now you need a friend to talk to, capisce?"

Charlee smiled at Peggy's vocabulary. Her father used to say that all the time to her. Was it an expression from the East Coast? From the military? She had no idea. "Well, it started the day I bought the typewriter."

CHAPTER 12

"Well, holy shit!" Peggy exclaimed after hearing Charlee tell her the whole story. Her eyes were wide with amazement. "Don't worry. I believe you. I don't think you're one of those hysterical, crazy types trying to get attention. How absolutely terrifying! It sounds like a scary movie! Ya know, I've heard before of ghosts attaching themselves to objects. It sounds like it's attached to the typewriter. But how crazy is that? I never saw anything here with it, except I always thought it was a little ugly and creepy and a dust collector. But what in the world..." Her voice trailed off incredulously.

"I know. It really sounds crazy! I'm so glad you believe me!" Charlie said a little breathlessly, feeling an enormous relief to unburden herself. "I haven't been sleeping or eating. I'm a basket case, and I can't tell my parents because they'll tell me 'I told you so!' They never wanted me to move to Oregon." She remembered the look of confusion and dismay on her parents' faces when she showed them the house in the real-estate magazine that she was planning on buying in Rogue River. Her mother had gone to bed with a migraine, and her father immediately headed toward the liquor cabinet and started drinking shots off his whiskey bottle. They had really put a damper on her enthusiasm.

"You're not alone, Charlee, and I'm glad you've moved to Oregon. Frankly, I think this is really interesting. Wow! I haven't heard anything this mysterious or exciting in ages! But we have to get a plan on figuring this out—research or exorcism or something." Her eyes sparkled with excitement.

"An exorcism?" Charlee laughed and threw her head back. And then they both laughed together with abandonment until tears ran down their faces. "I guess I needed that. I've been such a wreck with all of this. I pictured us in long robes, candles, and crosses while chanting something." And she began to giggle again. "I was brought up Catholic. I guess I should be more reverent," she said with a mischievous smile.

"Now that's my girl!" Peggy said following with a raucous laugh. "So where do we start?"

"Hmmm...Peggy, where did the typewriter come from? Who gave it to you?" Charlee's dark eyes were troubled and questioning. She pushed a long strand of dark hair away from her face that had escaped her ponytail and leaned forward expectantly.

"Well, I had it in my storage of all the stuff I collect, and I brought it out just about six months ago and put it in the shop here. Had a hell of a time lugging it in here by myself too." She took a sip of her coffee and bit into her doughnut. "Where is a man when you need one, right?" Her eyes gazed out searching into the past. Refocusing, she turned her head to Charlee and said, "I bought it from an estate sale many years ago."

"When you bought it, did they tell you anything about it?" Charlee's voice was almost a whisper, and she stifled a shiver that ran down her spine.

"Well, I remember the sale was here in Rogue River, not far from your house. I talked to a woman...looked like maybe she was in her thirties? Not sure. Her mother had died. She was getting rid of everything. I'm sorry. That's all I remember," Peggy said apologetically. Her eyes were filled with concern.

Charlee sat quietly for a moment. "Well, I guess that's something. At least you remember buying it, right? Can you remember how many years back it was?"

Peggy's face brightened. "Yes, ha! Actually, I do! It was the year we landed on the moon. It had just happened!" They both looked at each other with puzzled looks on their faces.

"I'm sure that probably means nothing. But at least the year came to me—1969."

"I wonder what I should do now. Maybe I should go to the library and look at the microfiche and search old newspaper articles. Would they cover estate sales? Maybe deaths though, right?" Charlee's voice was low, almost as if she was thinking aloud.

"You could be like a detective. Or I've got an idea—maybe ask that cute cop if he can help. What's his name? O'Malley? Have you seen him?" Peggy asked with a sly smile.

Charlee's felt her face flush. "Yeah, I've seen him. And you're right, he's pretty good-looking. But he'd think I was a crazy lady if I went into the police department squawking about a ghost. I'll start with the library first."

"Okay, but don't rule it out. He might have access to information that would take longer for you to discover. So no séance or exorcism?" Peggy's eyes twinkled with humor. She was glad that Charlee wasn't looking quite as distraught as when she entered.

"Yeah, maybe a séance. Know any good mediums?" Charlee laughed. She looked over at the door. Chewy's big nose was squashed up against the glass. He was trying to catch sight of her. When he knew he had her attention, he pulled away from the door. "Oh geez," Charlee said with a little exasperation, "look at that big sloppy spot he put on your door."

"Big as a teacup! Wow! He really is huge! Good thing you have him. Ya gotta feel safe with a dog that's as big as a horse! Don't worry about it. I'll clean it up later. You should go home and get some rest. You really do look exhausted."

"Yeah, okay. Thanks, Peggy, for listening to me. That helped. I'll see ya later." She opened the door, bells jangling noisily, and Chewy nodded his head up and down, relieved that she was coming out to him. "Okay, Chewy! Let's go home and start planning a ghost hunt."

CHAPTER 13

After she left Peggy, she realized she wasn't ready to go home yet. *Stalling? You bet!* she thought. They wandered through the town, window-shopping, and then took a long slow meandering walk along the riverbank. *Lonely is the one who walks the riverbanks looking for solace in the dead of winter,* she thought, a little morosely. *It really is very beautiful here, but these gray skies start to really get to you.* Chewy leaned his massive head against her leg and sighed. *Okay, time to snap out of it. I'm depressing my dog.*

The sky was beginning to darken, and she found herself back on Main Street. She strolled over to the little corner market and bought a can of clam-chowder soup, a loaf of French bread, and a bottle of Chardonnay. The clerk, an older man with a balding head, glasses, and a friendly smile rang up her items on the cash register and smiled. "All the things a girl needs, right?"

Charlee laughed and said, "Almost! Let's add this candy bar! Gotta have chocolate!" Charlee added the Heath bar to her items. Charlee left the store smiling and unleashed Chewy from the bike rack.

Together, they walked down the street in an easy stride until they hit Oak Street. Then, the pace began to slow down. Each step became slower and more measured the closer they got to their house. They stood outside the gate to the house, transfixed and not moving.

Charlee heaved a deep sigh. Chewy sat down and leaned his head forlornly against her side again. *I dread going in there! I really do! All of my bravado—what a farce! I'm terrified. All this crazy, spooky stuff that I can't even begin to explain or understand. I don't want to face this alone. I'm always alone! I don't know what to do. Maybe I should go home to Arrowhead. Why in the world am I here anyway? In this bleak little wet gray town?* With this last dismal thought, large raindrops began to spatter down. *Of course, more rain.* She continued to stand there staring at her house.

"Thinking of going in?" A voice behind her said with interest and a teasing tone. She hadn't heard the police car pull up beside her, and Chewy hadn't noticed either. She glared at Chewy for his lack of observation.

She turned slowly and smiled with a little chagrin. *I must look a little nuts, standing here staring at my house,* she thought. *Maybe some company would be nice for a change.* Deciding to be a little bold, she said, "I was waiting for you. You're late! I have soup, bread, and wine!" She lifted up her bag, smiled, and lifted one eyebrow questioningly.

"Charlee, I think you are a force to be reckoned with!" He laughed and got out of his car, nodding his dark curly head. "Good thing I'm off work now. I'd love some soup on this cold, rainy evening!" He followed her through the gate and up the stairs. "Wow! Look at your neighbor lady over there glaring at us!"

"Yeah, I don't think she likes me much. And does it ever stop raining?" Charlee said, changing the subject.

After Charlee had poured the wine, soup, and sliced up the French bread in nice slabs with butter and cheese on the side, they slipped into a comfortable teasing banter. Corbin told her he had grown up in Bend, Oregon, with his two brothers and dad on a ranch.

"A little like *Bonanza,*" he laughed. "I wasn't sure if I wanted to be a cowboy or a movie star, so I decided to be a cop instead. My dad was not so impressed with my decision." He smiled, his blue eyes sparkling with humor. "What's your story? Why are you here, Charlee?" he questioned with interest.

"I was drawn here for some reason. I don't really know why..." Her voice trailed off introspectively.

Suddenly, they were in darkness. The power had flickered and was out. Then it was back on, then off. On. Off. On. Off.

"What the hell?" Corbin said aloud with wonder. The lights continued to go on and off and stayed off. The temperature in the room dipped quickly. Charlee's face was ghostly pale with her lips parted, and her eyes were wide with fear. Chewy sidled up closer to them, emanating a low growl.

Corbin pulled his lighter from his pants and lit the candle on the table. He stood up, walking to the front door and peered out into the darkness. "Charlee, yours is the only house that doesn't have power. Electrical problems? Didn't pay the bill?" he tried to say jokingly. "Are you okay?" he questioned with concern.

Charlee looked stunned with fear. An interesting mixture of strength and vulnerability shined in her dark eyes. Something was wrong about this. "Maybe it's electrical." Her voice came out, nearly a whisper. Suddenly, the door to her office opened and slammed shut with a loud bang.

"Is somebody here?"

Charlee shook her head no. Corbin drew the gun from his holster, approached her office slowly, and quietly turned the knob, pushing the door open with a squeak. He swung the door the rest of the way open and peered inside. The streetlamp outside illuminated the room dimly. "There's no one here. All clear! But damn, it's freezing in here!"

The curtain over her desk suddenly billowed out, and the top drawer to her desk opened and then slammed shut. Then a rushed and whispery voice blasted out sharply, piercing the air, "I HAVE THE STORY!" Then silence. Steam rose off his breath as he whispered hoarsely, "What the hell? Is this place haunted or what?"

"Copy that!" Charlee giggled slightly hysterically.

CHAPTER 14

"Charlee, what the hell is going on here? You are as pale as a ghost and terrified! I know we just met, but you can talk to me. Please try and trust me..." He paused, staring into her face intently. Her eyes were fixed on his intently, searching.

She let out the breath that she had been holding unintentionally. "Okay. I will tell you the whole crazy, spooky story. If you laugh at me, I'll scream and throw you out of here. Ya got it?" She looked at him with a deadpan, serious face, and he knew she meant it.

He leaned back in his chair, took a large gulp of wine, and said, "Go ahead."

She proceeded and told him the whole story from the time she saw the house in the real-estate ad up until that very night. She decided to omit how unhappy and unsupportive her parents had been in her move to Oregon.

"So do you think I'm crazy and making all this stuff up?" She had lifted her chin in defiance, with one eyebrow raised and her eyes poring into him, and yet there was an air of sweet vulnerability about her.

Corbin, after listening to her story, wanted to reach out and hug her and tell her everything was going to be okay. Peggy had already told him everything that Charlee had told her, but he had to have Charlee tell her story herself. She had been through so much. Where were her parents, family, friends in all of this? Why was she alone? He looked into her defiant eyes. No, she didn't want a hug. He quietly told her, "I believe you, and I'll help you figure out what's going on. What do you want to do next?"

Charlie looked at him, a little surprised but relieved. "What I would like to do next is get one night of real sleep. I haven't slept a whole night in I don't know how long. Do you mind staying near, letting me sleep, and keeping the boogeyman away for a night?" she said with a teasing lilt in her voice.

"No problem, ma'am," he said with an exaggerated Southern drawl. He pushed her gently back on the couch and covered her gently with the quilt that lay nearby. He lightly gave her a peck on the forehead and smiled comfortingly at her. "It's okay. Just sleep. I'll be right over here in this chair. No worries now."

Something in his voice made her believe him, and she was out, snoring peacefully within minutes. Chewy lumbered over and settled down on the floor beside her and was snoring like crazy too. Chewy was exhausted too. He had been watching over Charlee like a security guard. He would give his life for her.

CHAPTER 15

Reluctantly, she opened her eyes to the brisk, cold morning air. It was still. Chewy lay at her feet, snoring gently. She had slept. She sat up wrapping the blanket around her tightly. Corbin was gone. *I hope he doesn't think I'm a total nut*, she thought as she reflected on the previous night. She smiled and shook her head. *He might be a little crazy himself if he doesn't think I am*, she thought with a giggle.

Looking around her living room, her furniture, her *Star Wars* paraphernalia, the useless little rock fireplace, she thought, *The house protects the dreamer. I am that dreamer! I am here for a reason. I was compelled to move here and buy this very crazy little haunted house. I am not a victim! I am not alone! I have Chewy! And I have Peggy who believes me, and I have maybe Corbin on my side, if he doesn't think I'm nuts, and I have*—she struggled for something else—*I have courage.*

Resolutely, she clambered off the couch, glancing at the empty wine and beer bottles and nearly gagging; stumbled into the bathroom; and turned on the shower. As she gathered her towel and put a new bar of soap in the dish, she looked over her shoulder at the steamy mirror and gasped. Words spelled out in the steamy mirror—I HAVE THE STORY!

She froze in position for a moment, staring at the mirror. *Nope! I'm not going to let that stop me! Nothing is going to stop me! Nothing!* To distract herself and keep up her bravado, she burst into song, singing "New York, New York," one of her father's Sinatra favorites. Her voice was a little off-key, but she just sang louder. Chewy pushed his way into the bathroom, poked his head around the shower curtain, and stared at her, tilting his head to one side. Charlee laughed and said, "Really, I'm not crazy. Just sound a little nuts!"

She gingerly stepped out of the shower, wrapped the towel around her, grabbed the little hand towel by the sink, and rubbed the dripping letters from the mirror. The bathroom was cold and filled with steam. She hastily applied her makeup, raced to her room, and pulled on her jeans and an oversized sweatshirt.

Purposefully, she went to the kitchen, made coffee, pulled out a pan, started frying two eggs, and dumped a can of dog food into Chewy's bowl. "We're going to need our strength, Chewy." Chewy stared into her eyes and seemed to understand. Charlee nodded. "You're damn straight we do!"

CHAPTER 16

With her hood flipped over her head to block the rain, Charlee and Chewy ran to her Jeep and hopped in quickly. "Whew! It's coming down!"

Within three minutes, she was pulling into the library. "Chewy, you gotta hang out here, okay? You're not allowed in a respectable, quiet place like a library, got it?" She smiled derisively. Chewy mournfully looked at her with drooping eyes and set his massive head upon his paws and settled into the seat.

Charlee ran inside with the door swinging shut behind her with a bang from a sudden gust of wind. The librarian, startled, looked up and smiled. "Well, hi! I didn't expect anyone so early with all this rain. Can I help you?"

Charlee, resolutely, walked to the counter. "I'm not sure how to go about this. But I was wondering if I could go through old newspapers or microfiche regarding events that have happened in this town for, well—crap! Ha! I don't know how many years!" She pushed her long hair behind her and smiled a very disarming smile. "I'm not sure exactly what I'm looking for, you see…I'm sorry. I don't mean to sound so mysterious," she said with a small laugh.

The librarian looked at her with fascination. "And I thought I was going to have a boring day! You are new here, right? I know I've never seen you in here before." She looked at Charlee with interest. This young woman, with her wild long auburn hair and flashing eyes, was bursting with an intensity that was held strongly in check.

"Yes, I'm still fairly new here and learning my way around. My name is Charlee Wilkes. I bought the little blue house on Oak Street. I'm trying to find some background information on the house and the town as well. Just trying to get information on local flavor or something. Does that make any sense to you?" She smiled sweetly and blinked her eyes.

The librarian led her to the back of the library to the microfiche machine. "I'll go and get some tablets and get this thing in gear for you. It's not too difficult once you get it going." Within ten minutes, she was back and showing Charlee how to insert the tablets and scroll back and forth through the articles.

Charlee settled down in her chair and started turning the knob. She browsed through weather reports; barroom brawls at the Homestead, the local bar in town; and lofty political aspirations. She stopped on a picture of a young couple smiling lovingly into the camera. The article stated that it was their wedding picture. They both had recently died in a car accident on West Evans Creek Road in Rogue River on July 4, 1950. Their four-month-old baby that was in the car had come up missing. There was no sign of an animal attack. The baby girl had vanished; and the grandfather was heartbroken, having lost his only daughter and granddaughter. The matter was under investigation with the police.

How very sad, Charlee mused thoughtfully. *They look so happy and hopeful in their picture.* She stared into their smiling faces—faces that were so unknowing of the near future. *To face such a disaster… and where did the baby go? The poor grandfather…such devastating loss…I'm really getting nowhere with my search. I'm just feeling sad. Oh well, I tried enough for today.* She thanked the librarian and walked back into the drizzling rain. The librarian gazed at her retreating figure thoughtfully.

She climbed into her Jeep, and Chewy raised his head and yawned widely. "Whew! You sure can stink up a car! Geez, I might pass out Chewy!" Her dog shifted his weight and looked at her indifferently over his shoulder and groaned.

She found herself pulling into the little Woodville Cemetery. She rolled the window down for Chewy and to air out the car. She somberly strolled through the cemetery and, once again, found herself at the little burial plot of the baby. The cracked angel statue remained loyally in place. *Such loss…* She thought of the young couple and the missing baby.

Looking up into the gray sky, her hair lifted gently with a breeze, and she shivered. Tears, unshed, misted her eyes. *I'm so alone here.* She looked dismally around the cemetery, all the little headstones standing straight as little soldiers at attention. A solitary black bird soared high in the air above her. *What in the world am I doing here? Why do I feel so alone? I have parents that love me and friends…* She thought of her parents. *Closed doors, I want to be safe. Why safe?* she wondered. *Why do I feel like an outsider looking in on my life? Am I as fragile as glass? Or crystal? Crystal shatters more beautifully than glass. Where have I heard that? What a crazy girl I am! Wouldn't I be fun for a psychologist?* She closed her eyes and held her face to the sky. Small drops of rain touched her face, almost apologetically. "Yes, it's time to go home," she chided herself. "You'll be very sorry if you get sick standing out in the rain in a graveyard."

CHAPTER 17

Sitting quietly on her couch and munching on her grilled-cheese sandwich and sipping her tomato soup from a large cup, she stared thoughtfully into the nonfunctional fireplace. *So nice if there were flames to reflect on,* she mused. *It might even be comforting.* Her right eyebrow lifted, and she smiled at the irony.

She stretched out her legs and wiggled her toes, imagining the warmth of a crackling fire. Chewy lifted his head and gave her a penetrating stare. *I need to get out more and meet some friends,* she thought. *I wish Corbin would have called or come by. He probably thinks I'm nuts. Hmmm...yes, this calls for a glass of wine.* She wrapped her throw blanket around her tightly and went into the kitchen. Pouring herself a large goblet of Merlot, she smiled and returned to her spot on the couch.

Turning on the TV to the news, she listened to President Jimmy Carter rambling on about international conflicts and peace. She snapped it off in boredom. It all felt so removed from her. *I'm in my own little Rogue River bubble,* she thought, *a guest in a ghost story—so strange, yes.* The wind in the trees seemed to whisper. Gusts of wind rattled the windows. She shivered.

"I'm putting this day to bed. What do you say, Chewy?" Lifting his magnanimous head, he seemed to nod in agreement and slowly lifted his bulky frame from the rug on the floor. They both clambered to her bedroom. Charlee pulled down the numerous blankets and quilts and slid in under all of them. Chewy looked at her questioningly.

"Yes, good Lord! You can sleep with me. Come on, you big lug!" Chewy, somehow gracefully, leaped over her and settled in beside her.

He gave a contented sigh, stretched out his legs, and placed his large head with a thump down on the feather pillow beside her. She smiled and looked lovingly into his bloodshot Saint Bernard eyes. "You're the best, Chewy!" She smiled and snuggled into his warmth.

CHAPTER 18

"Millions of stars...such a dark night, but all those stars...so far away...such a silent night—not a sound. Where am I?" She stretched her arms to the stars as if to grasp them in her inquisitive fingers. "Can anyone see me?" She carefully looked about, her eyes scanning. She looked down at her bare feet. "So strange. I need to move more quickly." She quickened her pace, walking uphill. And little pebbles dug into her bare feet, but it didn't matter. She felt nothing.

There was the sign—Woodville Cemetery. "So I'm here again." Silently, she glided down the path of the dead. Halting at the grave of the lost baby, she lifted her eyes to the large impervious full moon. By the light of the silvery moon, she thought, and tears welled in her dark eyes. She lifted the edge of her long white nightgown, raised her other arm in a gesture of a waltz, and twirled—twirling and dancing in circles, and more circles, and more circles. She began to sing in a soft murmur, "You are my sunshine, my only sunshine..." Out of breath, she stared down in shock at her nightgown, trailing in the rocks, dirt, and mud. "How am I dirty?" She covered her eyes with her hands and wept. Her tears ran through her fingers and, touching her wrists and gaining momentum, fell to the ground in tiny, little waterfalls.

"No!" she screamed, "why am I here now?" Her voice shattered the silence of the graveyard. A baby's voice screamed in terror, and she was running. Her feet were slapping the wet pavement wildly as she ran in the direction to her house.

"I must get home! I must get home!" Her voice was in constricted sobs. She could hear the baby's screams echoing behind her.

"Oh my God! Why am I leaving a screaming baby! I don't know! I don't know!" She continued running. There was no one on the streets to witness her hysteria—just the moon and all those damn stars looking down at her, disinterested and disenchanted.

She bolted through her front door and stopped abruptly. A slight man's figure stood in front of her with his back turned to her. Words froze in her throat. She stood motionless. There was not a sound. No dog barking. "Where was Chewy?" She exhaled slowly, and her breath came out in soft clouds of steam—so cold. Her terror escalated in her mind, screaming and screaming but not a word escaped her lips. It's true. When you're terrified, you can't scream. The man's clothing hung loosely on his frame. He was motionless. He had a hat on his head, one worn during Bogart's time. These thoughts blazed through her mind. She could feel electricity in the air and could sense the tiny hairs on her body rising. She shut her eyes tightly and wished him away.

Opening her eyes, he was still there. He was beginning to move. His right hand slowly lifted to his head, and gingerly, he removed the hat. Blood dripped down his head and onto his shoulders. His skull was caved in, and a white pulsing gore bulged from the confines of bone. In shocked horror and macabre fascination, she stood transfixed, unable to scream or utter a word.

Slowly he turned. His dark deep-set eyes stared mournfully at her. He had a face of torture and eyes that held so much pain. The deep lines on his face showed the ravages of unmerciful time. She stared into his eyes, mesmerized and feeling as if she would faint. The room shifted beneath her feet. He stretched out a hand to her and whispered, "I have the story! I have the story! I have the story!" His face was so intent and his voice so desperately pleading. His voice rose in a crescendo. "I HAVE THE STORY!"

His voice was screaming in her ears, and then she heard the wailing of the baby coming closer and closer. They blended into two long wailing sounds, a cacophony of chaotic blended noise, and the room was moving quickly around her. She sat down on the floor, covered her head with her arms, pulled her nightgown around her as a shield, and screamed, and screamed, and screamed.

CHAPTER 19

Strong arms were lifting her. She felt herself lowered into blankets and realized dimly that she was on her couch. A hand was gently tapping her cheek. "Are you okay? Are you hurt? What happened?" She felt her head raised and a glass tipped to her lips. "Here, drink this." Warm brandy slid down her throat, and she lifted her eyes and saw Corbin's worried face looking down at her.

There were other people in the room, waiting expectantly for her to answer. Charlee blinked, looked around, and hesitated. "I think she's okay. Thanks for sounding the alert. You can go back home now," Corbin said with an authoritative voice. He shut the front door quietly behind the retreating figures.

"Charlee, what the hell happened? Your neighbor lady called the department and said you were screaming like you were being murdered. Chewy was howling and galloping around the room, knocking things over. She saw you lying on the floor, and she thought she saw blood. Damn! Are you okay? I got here as fast as I could. You were out cold, and you're covered in mud! What the hell? For the love of God, say something!" Corbin stared at her in frightened exasperation.

Charlee's white face stared at him in shock. "I saw him," she stammered. "I saw the ghost. It was awful. Blood and brains and his skull crushed in...it was horrible—such haunting deep dark eyes. He was screaming at me. Somehow, he knows me. I don't understand." She shivered convulsively, clenching onto his hand with ferocious strength, and tears began to flow down her cheeks. "Such desolation, such loss...he looked into me. He knew me. I don't understand. He was trying to tell me something, and there was a baby screaming..."

Her voice trailed off, and she stared into the vast memory of her recent horror.

Corbin could see that she was in shock, and he placed another blanket around her shoulders and brought the glass of brandy to her lips again. Chewy sat nearby in a state of hypervigilance.

"Charlee, sweetie, why is your nightgown covered in mud? Where did you go?"

"I dreamt I was at the cemetery, and I was dancing. A baby, a dead one, started screaming, and I ran away. I ran from a baby screaming. There was rain and the moon. And I ran. Why would I do that? But mud? It was a dream! Then I was home, and he was here with the blood—" Her voice choked off with a stifled sob.

"Hush! Don't think of it anymore tonight. I'll stay here for the night. It's gonna be okay." He rushed into her room, rifled through her drawers, and pulled out another nightgown. He brought it to her, and she lifted her arms in exhausted obedience to the replacement. He laid her head gently back on the couch pillow. He re-covered her gently with her afghan blanket, and Chewy looked on with concern and appreciation.

He poured himself a large glass of brandy and settled himself into the armchair. Charlee was already asleep, and he looked protectively into her pale and haunted face. Then his gaze was drawn to a wet spot on the floor. *More mud?* He went to the kitchen and got a paper towel. Bending down, he wiped it up, and bringing it into the light, he gasped. Blood!

CHAPTER 20

She awakened slowly and reluctantly to the sound of rain lightly pattering on the roof top. The room was quiet, except for the ticking of the clock. She pulled the quilt and afghan more tightly around her and shivered. Chewy was lying on the floor next to her, his big sad eyes watching her carefully.

"I'm sorry, Chewy. You sure saw a lot of crazy last night, huh?" Her voice sounded a little hoarse and breathless. From all that screaming she thought. The terrifying memories flashed through her mind, and she pushed them away. *What in the world do I do next? My neighbors must think I'm batshit crazy, and Corbin is probably getting a little burnt out on this spooky drama too. I bet he was glad to go to work this morning.* She glanced at the clock; it was 9:15 a.m. *I feel like I could lie here all day. Hmmm…what's inspiring me to get up though is my bladder. Damn.* She stiffly walked to the bathroom, bumping into furniture as she went.

Looking into the bathroom mirror, she gasped. "Wow! I look like crap!" Her long curly auburn hair was sticking out wildly in a tangled mess. Her mascara had run and created dark circles under her eyes. *I'm glad Corbin is gone. I look as wild and spooky as my ghost! Ha! Now, it's my ghost.* She stared into the mirror at her dark, tired, and haunted eyes. *The ghost's eyes were so dark, tortured, and insistent. He really wanted to tell me something. It's all so frightening and mysterious.*

Going into the kitchen, she put on a pot of coffee and dumped Chewy's food in his bowl. He enthusiastically started slurping it down. She marveled at his never-ending appetite. She cracked a few eggs in a pan and put some bread in the toaster. She wasn't hungry, but she felt a little weak. So she knew it was time for food and protein.

Quietly she sat eating her breakfast, looking out the window and watching the rain relentlessly drown the world outside. The trees looked so forlorn and bare of all their leaves. A light wind was blowing, and the trees seemed to shiver with the breeze. She stared at the large solitary oak in her yard. *Such a strong and magnificent oak tree. It has faced so many winters and will long after I'm gone.*

Why has the ghost remained here in this world? Why didn't it cross over into heaven or hell? Unfinished business? It seemed so tormented and desperate to tell her something. It seemed like it knew her. *But that doesn't make sense. How could it know me? Those eyes. Those tormented eyes.*

Suddenly she noticed a folded piece of paper on the corner of the table. It was a note from Corbin. Her mind stilled, expecting the worst. She slowly unfolded it. "Charlee, I hope you're feeling better this morning. I cleaned up the blood on the floor with paper towels. Were you hurt? I hadn't noticed anything last night. Try not to worry. We'll figure this out. I'll talk to you later. Corbin."

She swiftly got out of her chair and opened the cupboard below the kitchen sink and pulled out the trash can. There was a wad of wet paper towels. No blood. How strange! *What is he talking about?* The only blood she remembered was the gore and blood on the ghost. She shuddered. Feeling a little creeped out and apprehensive, she looked around the room. *It's so still; it feels like the house is watching me, or something is.* A feeling of expectancy and hypervigilance.

Reflectively, she sat back down at the table and stared out the window. *I have several options here: I could bail out of here, sell the house, and go back to my parents and live with them; sell the house and buy another in the area; or buck up and find out who this ghost is and why he's here. Well, I'm not a quitter, so I guess it's time to buck up.* She picked up her plate of half-eaten eggs, resolutely pushed herself away from the table, dumped her plate in the sink, and headed to her room to get ready for the day. As she passed her office, the door gently opened with a low squeak.

CHAPTER 21

Pulling the hood up on her sweatshirt as far as she could and hiding her face, she slipped out the front door. Chewy was quietly slinking up behind her. *I feel like some kind of criminal sneaking around*, she thought. *If Chewy could tiptoe, he would*, she thought with amusement.

And then, of course, with the bang of a front door opening, there was her neighbor Wilamena. "Charlee, oh Charlee! Yoo-hoo! Are you okay after last night? I'd like to talk to you! Hey! I know you heard me! Come back! I want some answers!"

Charlee swiftly walked down the street away from her relentless and nosy neighbor. She took a deep breath as she hit Main Street. *Whew! I know she probably means well, but that woman drives me crazy!* She quickly headed over to Peggy's antique shop. The air was brisk and cold and stung her cheeks. *I need to talk to Peggy.*

Peggy was always kind, laughing, and very down to earth. She tied Chewy up outside and swung open the door, bells jangling, and she heard a *ho ho* of a Santa. *Wow! It really is almost Christmas.*

Peggy looked up at her with a smile and said, "Hi, spooky, haunted lady! I heard all about it! Corbin was in earlier, and you've had a few neighbors buzz through here. The nosy old bats!"

Charlee had been walking in, feeling embarrassed, and sporting a hangdog look, but when Peggy had burst out with her greeting, Charlee put back her head and laughed. Peggy joined in with her laughter.

"So what now, sweetie? What do you want to do next?"

After she had relayed the whole experience to Peggy—blood and brains and everything—she said, "I need to get this figured out.

I need to find out who has lived there since the house was built and go from there. I have to stop being a scared child, or I might as well go home to my parents and admit defeat. And frankly, I really, really don't want to do that. Hell no!"

Charlee was trembling and exhausted, but the look in her eyes was determined. Her long curly dark hair was loose and wildly sticking out in every direction. It gave her a fierce and volatile air.

She really is beautiful and a force to be reckoned with, Peggy thought with admiration. "Well, okay then, let's call the tax accessor in Medford. Those blood suckers know everything, right? Bastards!" she said with a raucous laugh.

Peggy pulled out the telephone book beside her antique cash register and looked up the number for the tax accessor for Jackson County. After the line rang several times, Peggy said, "Hello, I'm calling for some information on an address in Rogue River. The address is 206 Oak Street. I believe it was built in early 1900. I'd like to know all the names of the people that owned this house up until the present. Can you get me that information? You can? That's wonderful! Thank you so much!" She winked at Charlee.

"Holy shit! Hand me that tablet, Charlee, quickly!" Charlee could hear a lady's voice on the other line, and Peggy was writing down names rapidly. "Okay, I got it! Thanks for your time!" Peggy sat triumphantly back with her paper in hand. "Do you love me or what?" She smiled impishly.

"Oh my Lord! Hand that over to me! Who are the names?"

Peggy held the piece of paper firmly. "I will read them to you. Okay, here it goes: Herman Strauss from 1910 till 1940, he built the house apparently; then David Kelly from 1941 to 1947; then Leopold Chaput from 1948 to 1951; and then Melanie Hamilton from 1952 to 1976. And then it is you. Get anything from this? We could maybe have Corbin research the names, right?" Peggy tilted her head to one side and looked at her quizzically. "Well?"

"Thank you, Peggy! Hopefully this helps. You know, one of those names sounds kinda familiar. Leopold Chaput. It seems like I've seen that name somewhere or something," she spoke aloud reflectively. "I think I'll go back to the library first. Don't tell anyone where I am," she said as she quickly strode to the front door.

"No problem, Sherlock," Peggy said with a wry smile.

CHAPTER 22

"Hi! I'm back! Could I please browse through your microfiche again?" Charlee asked as she breezed through the doorway. Her long auburn curls swirled around her face, and energy emanated from her small form. Her gaze was already fixed on the next room where the machine was located.

The librarian looked up with a smile, "Well, of course you can! Nice to see you again! How do you like our little town? Are you getting settled into your new house?"

"Yeah, I think I am, and it is a friendly little town. Would you mind setting me up on the microfiche that I looked at the last time I was here? I'd like to look at some of those articles again."

"An article in particular?" she asked with a little curiosity. She looked at Charlee with interest. She had heard some talk in town that Charlee had had the police called to her house and was often seen walking alone along the river. In fact, she had heard a cop car was parked out her house numerous times at all hours of the night. Hmmm… It was a small town, and news traveled fast.

"Maybe, not sure yet," Charlee said in an abstracted manner. "The microfiche?" She didn't want to waste a minute on trivial chitchat.

"Oh yes, of course! I'll go and get it." She bustled off and returned shortly, setting it up in the machine. She reminded Charlee how to scroll though the articles. She slowly and reluctantly walked away. *I wonder what she is so curious about. She is an interesting person, maybe a little secretive. I wonder why the police went to her house last night. Hmm…news travels fast in a small town*, she thought again.

Charlee settled into her seat and began scrolling through the articles. She wasn't sure exactly what she was searching for but felt that she would know it when she saw it. Article after article flashed before her eyes. *This could give you a headache,* she thought with exasperation. Then the article of the young smiling couple that had been killed in an auto accident flashed on the screen. *Whoa! Wait a minute.* She looked closely at the couple's faces. *How very sad—so young. And how strange. The baby went missing.* She started to reread the article and then stopped abruptly. The parents' names were Andre and Elise Deveraux, and Elise was survived by her father Leopold Chaput.

Are you kidding me? Her pulse raced, and her breath caught in her throat. Charlee quickly grabbed her purse and took out the names that were written down at Peggy's shop. Her purse fell on the floor and items fell out and rolled away on the shiny surface. Her lipstick rolled three feet away from her. The librarian leaned as far as she could in her chair to see what was happening.

Quickly she unfolded the paper, and there was the name Leopold Chaput. "Holy shit!" she exclaimed with surprise. She stared at the name in astonishment. She felt a chill and looked down at her arms, now covered in goose bumps and all the little hairs standing at attention. *What does this mean? I'm living in the house of this Chaput guy who was the grandfather of the baby that went missing, whose parents died in a car crash. Weird! But it is a small town and all. Should it mean anything?* She stared back up at the smiling faces on the screen.

"Is everything okay?" the librarian called out inquisitively.

"Oh yeah, it's okay. Everything is fine! I just saw something that surprised me a little bit," Charlee said a little breathlessly. She pulled herself out of the chair and picked up the items from her purse and stuffed them back in a little haphazardly. The librarian was still looking at her quizzically, but Charlee ignored her and went back to staring at the picture on the screen.

A million questions were swirling around in her brain. *Could this Chaput guy be the ghost? The ghost was a man. How does it connect with the typewriter? And the ghost keeps saying and typing "I have the story!" What in the world does that mean? And...the baby crying...* She felt a chill race up her spine. The blood, the gore, and those dark deep-set haunted eyes rose up in her mind's eye. He was trying to tell her something terrifying! *And...I don't get it! Whack!* She slapped her hand down on the table like a definitive exclamation point. The librarian's head snapped up with the sound.

"I can't do this anymore right now!" Charlee exclaimed as she swung her purse over her shoulder and strode out the front door.

"Okay, dear..." the librarian's voice trailed off. She continued to watch Charlee over the edge of her glasses that hung down low over her nose. Bemusedly continuing to gaze out, she watched Charlee untie Chewy from the bicycle stand, toss her long hair behind her, and stride off quickly down the street. Chewy picked up his pace to keep up with her. *There is something a little strange about that girl,* she thought to herself.

CHAPTER 23

Kicking the gravel out under her feet in her haste while leaving the library, Charlee forced herself to slow down. *I don't want to look like a crazy lady running down the street dragging a Saint Bernard. But what should I do? What should I do right now? Should I go talk to Corbin at the police station?* In her mind's eye, she pictured the looks of interest on people's faces if she walked into the station—and maybe the smirks. She bit her lip and shook her head. *Nope.* She couldn't go in there right now. *Ha! And I should give Corbin a little break too. I'll go back to Peggy. Maybe she can help me get a grasp on this.*

"Sorry, Chewy," she said as she retied him at the door outside Peggy's shop. Chewy turned his mournful eyes on her and then turned his face away. *That dog can make me feel so guilty*, she thought. She pushed open the door to the jingling bells and the *ho ho* greetings from Santa. "That Santa is getting on my nerves!" She called out to Peggy.

"I know, right?" Peggy laughed. "I had you in mind when I put him up." Peggy was hanging ornaments on a tree and was standing on a ladder, trying to reach the top branches.

"You're so little. You just need an elf suit!" Charlee laughed. She looked at Peggy fondly. The vast difference in their ages meant nothing. She really liked this high-spirited little lady. "I need to talk to you and tell you what I found out." Her face now held a pensive and worried look.

"Okay, okay! But look who's calling who little, ha!" She clambered down the ladder, went over to her small desk behind the counter, and poured them both a cup of coffee. She turned to Charlee, ruffled her hands through her short curly locks, and gave her full attention.

"What in the hell did you find out? I can tell you found out something. It's written all over your face." She leaned forward and waited expectantly.

After relating all that she had discovered at the library, she asked, "So what do you think? Kinda crazy connection, right? Ya think he's my ghost? I thought of going to Corbin at the cop shop but changed my mind. Didn't want to have anybody looking at me like I'm crazy, ya know? I don't mean Corbin, but ha! He might think I'm a little nuts by now." She smiled with derision.

Peggy nodded understandingly. She looked steadfastly at Charlee and said, "I say we go to your house together right now and call this son of a bitch out! He says he has a story and keeps scaring the crap out of you. Well, no more! It's time for him to tell his damn story!"

She nodded her head sharply and smacked her hand down on her desk. A little blue porcelain bird on her desk toppled over on its side. Peggy laughed. "I think I gave it a heart attack!"

Charlee's dark eyes were wide with amazement, "Seriously? Right now? You want to confront my ghost?" She inwardly groaned at the use of *my ghost*. "What about the neighbors? They are still reeling in shock from all my crazy last night! They think I'm totally out there!" Her mind was spinning, and she had to admit she felt embarrassed. She twirled a lock of her hair nervously.

"The neighbors! Are you shittin' me? Who cares about them? Really? Come on! Let's do it now! I'm with you!" Abruptly she stood up, grabbed her jacket, and motioned toward the door. She tilted her head and said in a teasing and quiet voice, "I double-dog dare you!"

"Okay, you're on! I never could resist a double-dog dare! Ha!" Charlee strode to the front door and called over her shoulder, "I'll meet you there! Wait a few minutes before you go because I'm walking with Chewy." With a parting *ho ho* from Santa, she walked out the door. "Shut up, Santa!" She could hear Peggy laughing at the rear of the store.

CHAPTER 24

She had just reached her front yard as Peggy drove up in her Ford, a three-quarter-ton pickup truck. Watching Peggy inch her way down the side of the truck and hop to the ground, Charlee shook her head in amazement. "I never would have pictured it! You look like a midget hopping down from that monstrosity!" Her eyebrows were raised, and a smile lit her face.

"Hey! Don't knock it! I need something big when I'm out scavenging garage sales for antiques." Peggy lowered her voice. "I think I just saw your neighbor peering through her front window," she said mischievously. Sure enough, the curtains moved, and they could see Wilamena peeking out at them.

"She really needs a hobby," Charlee said, shaking her head. She looked at Peggy with a serious look, "Are you sure you want to do this? I'm really not sure what's gonna happen when we go in there. It might be nothing, and then you can think maybe I'm nuts. Or it could scare the wits out of you." She held her gaze with Peggy and concern was in her eyes.

Unblinking, Peggy stared right back and said, "Seriously, I can do this. Stop being such a worrier. I'm tougher than I look."

And with that, they headed up the stairs, Chewy following cautiously and warily behind them. As they reached the top step, the front door swung open slowly with a low squeak.

CHAPTER 25

Peggy took Charlee's hand as they walked through the door. Both of their eyes were wide and their steps tentative. The temperature dropped dramatically, and their breath blew in silver haloes around them. Peggy's voice tremulously squeaked out, "I care about my friend here, and you have been really scaring her! Are you this guy Chaput? What are ya doing?" The lights flickered on and off. Chewy began to growl, his hair rising on his haunches. Above their heads, in the attic, there was a loud, clumping sound as if something fell over and then the sound of feet running back and forth. A baby's cry suddenly pierced the air, and Peggy and Charlee clung to each other in terror. *What is it with a baby crying?* Charlee wondered in terror. The curtains started to billow out around the room, and the newspapers on the coffee table blew up in the air by an unseen force of power.

Charlee screamed out, "Damn it! You say you *have the story*. What is the *story?*" Suddenly everything stopped. The newspapers fell to the table. The curtains were motionless. It was still freezing cold. Chewy warily looked at her and held his gaze. Then, the whole house started shaking as if it was an earthquake. Pictures fell from the wall, dishes toppled over, and the sounds of breaking glass. The door to her office slammed open, and Charlee, hanging on desperately to Peggy's hand, slowly walked toward the open door.

In shock, they watched the typewriter clacking away quickly, the return going back and forth over the page as if by an invisible hand. The keys were moving rapidly. They inched closer and a little bit closer. Charlee, terrified, stretched her neck to see what was being typed on the paper. Breathlessly, she stared in shock at the typed message.

MURDERMURDERMURDERMURDER
MURDERMURDERMURDERMURDER.

It was typed over and over again—line after line—furiously typed with no breaking points. It continued to type and type. Charlee and Peggy stared in horror. At the end of the page, it still furiously continued to type.

Charlee felt Peggy slump beside her and slowly sink to the floor. "Oh my God! Peggy, are you okay?" She looked at Peggy's pale face and fear-stricken, frozen eyes. She dragged her to the living room and felt her pulse. *Oh God, I think she's had a heart attack! What do I do? Good Lord! What do I do?* She rushed over to the telephone and dialed for the operator. "Operator! Connect me to the hospital! I need an ambulance immediately!"

She grabbed a blanket and put it over Peggy and placed a pillow under her head. Gasping and crying, she said, "Oh Peggy, I'm so sorry. You've been such a good friend! Please! Please! Be okay! I can't lose you now. There are so few in my corner as you have been. Please hang in there! Please! Dear God! Please watch over this little lady!" The house was silent and listening. Chewy hovered over the both of them, his eyes scrutinizing the area and searching.

She was sobbing and clinging to Peggy as the ambulance came. They pulled her gently from her and told her what hospital they were taking Peggy to. Peggy looked so small and gray faced as they put her on the gurney. She looked apologetically into Charlee's eyes. Charlee stared back pleadingly. Peggy was loaded onto the ambulance. The sirens wailed, and she was gone. Alone, Charlee stood there until it was out of sight. She felt an arm grasp her shoulder, and Corbin was suddenly there, holding her in his arms and telling her it would be all right. "And what the hell happened anyway?"

"I may have lost the best friend I've ever had." She took him by the hand and led him back to her office. She showed him the type-written page. His hand clutched hers tightly—his blue eyes wide—and in a low, quiet voice, he said, "Murder?"

CHAPTER 26

"Oh my God! Oh my God! Please be okay!" Charlee whispered aloud. She was driving carefully but quickly to the hospital. "Be alert and stay focused," she admonished herself. Chewy sat in the front seat beside her, giving her support with his quiet ways.

Quickly she turned into the emergency parking lot, threw open her door, and said, "Chewy, I'll be back soon. Stay calm!" She realized saying *stay calm* was really meant for herself. Her heart pounding, she strode to the entrance and the receptionist desk. "I'm here for Peggy," she said breathlessly and gave her name.

"Yes, she was just brought in. Please wait over there. There is coffee if you like. We will call you up to see her as soon as we can." The receptionist smiled in her professional way and indicated what Charlee should do.

Charlee moved forward and woodenly sat in a chair facing the receptionist. In the emergency waiting room, her eyes moved from one stricken face to another—all waiting. Will it be bad or good news? A toddler was running around unattended, and a baby was crying. A young man was pacing back and forth, and an old woman was sitting dejectedly in a corner, hands clasped in prayer. *This is the reality of life*, Charlee thought sadly.

"Charlee Wilkes!" The nurse announced her name; and Charlee ran to the door, following the attendant. She was ushered back to a small room where Peggy was lying in a bed with numerous monitors attached to her. She looked so tiny, as small as a child; pale; helpless; defenseless; and so fragile. She felt the air sucked out of her lungs. Enormous waves of guilt engulfed her. "Oh my God, Peggy!' she whispered aloud.

Slowly she walked up to Peggy and grasped her hand that was lying outside the blanket. Peggy turned her head to her and weakly smiled, "We need to learn a lot more about exorcism, right?"

"Peggy, I'm so sorry. I'm an idiot! Never should have brought you into the crazy!" She tried to smile, but her voice cracked. Her eyes were large with grief.

Peggy grasped her hand firmly and looked into her eyes, "Stop that! You be tough. There's a lot more ahead with this. Be strong! Figure this out with Corbin. He will help you. Take it one step at a time. I'll be okay. I'll take this one day at a time. I will get better. I'm gonna hate the food here..." Her voice trailed off as she closed her eyes. Charlee stared at her quiet face. *Is this the last time I will see her alive?*

Charlee sat and waited for the doctor to tell her to leave and that she could check in with her tomorrow. As she was leaving, Peggy's husband and daughter were entering to check on her. They exchanged puzzled glances. *Funny, I never thought of her as married. She never talks of her family. We always talk about my crazy world. Am I that self-centered?* she wondered.

The rain was pouring down as she raced to her car. Chewy looked at her sadly with his big brown eyes. She lowered her head to the steering wheel and cried heart-wracking sobs. *What was all of this about? Why was she here? What the hell is this ghost thing? My friend may be dying! And I'm some crazy, selfish brat who caused all of it! Life is so flipping fragile.* She lifted her teary face to Chewy, who gave her a big slurpy, juicy kiss on her cheek. "Oh man! What do I do next?" she wondered aloud.

"Hey, Corbin! Can Chewy and I crash at your house tonight?" She waited breathlessly after dialing his number, not sure that he was back home yet or not. "I just can't go back into my crazy ghost house tonight."

"Where are you?" Corbin asked, his voice sounding worried.

"I'm calling from some grubby little pay phone on Rogue River Highway."

The rain was pounding loudly on the metallic roof. There was a motel nearby, and she could hear a drunken couple yelling and swearing at each other outside their room in the parking lot. *Just shut up!* She wanted to scream. She sniffed and wiped the tears from her eyes.

"Are you crying? Is...Peggy okay?" he asked with a growing lump in his throat. Peggy had been a good friend to him since he moved into Rogue River two years ago. He knew Charlee was very attached to her too. Peggy was the salt of the earth, and he really cared about her.

"I think so...I don't know. She says she will be," she mumbled sadly. "Her husband and daughter are with her now."

Feeling relieved and taking a deep breath, he said, "Of course you can come here. It's hard to hear you. Sure is a racket around you. Sounds like hell." The screaming couple was now slamming car doors, and there was a sound of breaking glass. "Just come straight here. I live at the top of Broadway on Valley View. It's a little red two-story house on the right. I'll have a glass of wine and a sandwich waiting for you. We have a lot to talk about."

"Okay, copy that." She forced a smile into her voice. "I'll be right there."

"Drive safely."

"Nope," she said teasingly.

"You sure are incorrigible," he said with a laugh as he hung up the phone.

CHAPTER 27

As she slowly pulled up to his house, she smiled. The red two-story house was lit up warmly, and there was smoke coming from the chimney. *What an inviting and charming house!* She stepped out of her car and immediately into a mud puddle. *But of course!* She smiled ruefully. "Come on, Chewy!" she beckoned. With enthusiasm, Chewy leaped from the car.

Before she knocked on the door, Corbin opened it with a smile and handed her a glass of wine. "Hey there! Come on in! I have a sandwich ready for you, and I put something together for Chewy."

He led her into the kitchen, and on the counter waiting for her was a sandwich with chips and salad. He put a large bowl down on the floor for Chewy who, with gusto, started slurping down its contents. "I don't know how you afford to feed that guy!" he laughed.

"This is really nice of you! I'm afraid I don't have any things with me, just my spooky self," she said apologetically with a small smile. She looked around his house with admiration. "This is such a nice place. You have great taste." The dining room had an oak table with four chairs and a hutch filled with china and tapestries hanging on the walls. The kitchen was cozy with brick walls and modern appliances. The fire glowed warmly from the living room.

"Thanks! I've been working on one room at a time. Come on now. Eat up!" He chatted on, telling her that he had picked up pieces of furniture and artwork from Peggy over the past two years and had even gone on a few estate sales with her. "I sure hope she'll be okay," he mused aloud. They both nodded in agreement. Peggy was special to both of them.

When she finished eating, Corbin picked up her plate, placed it in the sink, and led her into the living room, grabbing the bottle of wine as he went.

"Now this is nice," Charlee said as she sank down into the couch, kicking off her wet shoes. Corbin laid a blanket over her lap. They both stared into the fire and absorbed the warmth from the crackling flames.

Corbin leaned over and refilled her glass. "I know we need to talk about ghosts, murder, and all that stuff, but how about we wait till morning to get a grip on that? I think it's time to relax and regain strength. It's been a crazy day today, right? What do you say?"

Charlee smiled appreciatively, "Yes, I most certainly agree. I can't even wrap my head around it right now." She stared into the fire reflectively. Everything in her life right now seemed hard to fathom. She felt there were answers just outside her grasp—and more questions as well.

Corbin reached over behind his end table and pulled out a guitar. "Would you care for a little serenading?" he questioned with a flirtatious smile. He strummed a few bars. A curl of his dark hair fell over his face, which was a little flushed from the wine and the heat from the fire.

"I would love to hear you play! You are full of surprises!" She smiled with admiration and rapt attention.

He continued strumming and started singing the song "Toulouse Street" by the Doobie Brothers. His voice was strong and low as he sang, "I'm walking in shadows I cannot see/Faces, they smile when I fall or flee/I just might pass this way again. I just might pass this way again."

Such a haunting and beautiful song, she thought. Mesmerized, she stared into the fire listening to his lulling voice.

Corbin watched Charlee's head bob and sink down to her chest. *Poor thing is wiped out*, he thought. He gently pushed her down on the couch and covered her with the blanket. He moved over to the armchair and patted Chewy's head. Chewy groaned and stretched his large body in front of the fire. Corbin reached for his guitar, sipped his wine, and continued to strum quietly.

CHAPTER 28

Sunlight streamed through the dining room window and into the living room, striking Charlee straight in her opening eyes. She looked around getting her bearings. "Chewy," she whispered. Chewy lifted his head. He was just a few feet from where she lay on the couch. He inched closer to her and placed his large head on her lap. She could hear coffee percolating from the kitchen and its rich aroma lifting in the air. She sat up and tried to smooth down her long tangled hair. *I must look like a wreck,* she thought.

"Hey, good morning, sunshine!" Corbin peeked his head into the living room, smiling and holding out a coffee cup for her. Charlee noticed he was dressed and freshly showered.

"No good morning sunshine," she said with a scowl but smiled and held out her hand for the coffee. She pulled the blanket around her snugly. "Looks like you had to tuck me in again. Sorry, I'm such lousy company," she said, smiling weakly.

"No problem. Actually, it was quite entertaining. Did you know you snore like Darth Vader's breathing?" he said laughing, imitating the breathy, whispery sound.

"No way!" Charlee threw back her head and laughed without restraint. Corbin joined in, and they laughed in unison. Chewy watched them carefully, his head following them back and forth. He wagged his tail and barked happily.

"Come on. Get up, and I'll make you some bacon and eggs. You can take a shower after that, if you like," he said, striding off to the kitchen. Charlee followed him, and when she got to the kitchen, she looked out the sliding door.

"Holy shit! What a view!" She opened the door and stepped out onto the deck. The view was panoramic of all the hills and the little town of Rogue River lying below. The clouds were breaking in the sky, and a rainbow was in the distance. She breathed in deeply the fresh air and smiled. "I could sit out here all day and figure out the universe."

"The view sold me on the place," Corbin said as he walked up behind her. "It really is beautiful, isn't it? I come out here all the time to just think, look at the stars, play my guitar, and yes, figure out the universe," he said with a smile, his blue eyes twinkling. He gave her hair a playful tug.

"Yes, I can picture you doing that. Let's eat! I'm starving! So are you a good cook too?" She sat down at the counter as he set her plate before her and poured them both more coffee. Corbin placed a plate down for Chewy too, and he was ravenously chowing down on it. They ate their breakfast quietly, knowing the moment was coming when they had to talk about the inevitable.

Corbin picked up their dishes, placed them in the sink, and poured more coffee. He sat down facing her, his eyes serious. "So let's talk about murder."

Charlee gulped on her coffee, nearly choking.

CHAPTER 29

Charlee relived the events at her house on the previous day up to Peggy being taken away in the ambulance. Corbin listened intently to the whole story without interrupting. "So you said you heard a sound in the attic and a baby crying. Hmm...I think we need to check out the attic, but I wonder what the crying baby means and how it fits into this," he said seriously.

"Yeah, weird. The sound in the attic was kind of a bumping, scraping sound. And the baby screaming was like what I heard in the graveyard. I've heard it a few times now. I wonder how it's related. The murder, I would think, is this Chaput guy, or maybe he murdered the guy with the head bashed in? That was a horrible, gruesome sight," she said with a shiver, remembering the haunted face.

"Are you up to it? Can you handle going back in there yet? If you can't, I'll just go by myself and see if I can find anything that would give us a clue. You could sit out on the deck, drink wine, and figure out the universe if you like," he said with a grin.

"Of course I'm up to it! This is my house and my ghost, and I've got to figure this out! Besides, I have you and Chewy to back me up. What's there to be afraid of, right?" she said with false bravado. She smiled triumphantly and said, "I'm going to take a shower right now, and I'll be ready in a jiff." She tossed her hair over her shoulder and headed to the bathroom. Before she closed the bathroom door, she called out," I really won't take long, so be ready to go ghost hunting."

Corbin followed behind Charlee's Jeep in his little white Datsun pickup truck. He noted she was slowing down a bit the closer she got to her house. *I sure hope we can figure something out today in broad daylight that isn't too terrifying*, he thought. *She has been through a lot, and I know this is wearing on her. I wonder why her parents are not involved in this at all. She rarely mentions them.* He pulled up behind her and joined her on the sidewalk in front of her house. He saw the curtains move in the house next door. *Geez, that nosy neighbor, Wilamena.*

"Ready?" He gave her hand a reassuring squeeze as they approached the door. She nodded solemnly. The door opened slowly and swung back with a squeak. They both looked at each other, wide-eyed.

"Damn. I hate it when it does that!" she swore under her breath.

"Yeah, really. It sure does add to the creepiness." They walked into the quiet house. The room temperature quickly plunged. Chewy, who was following behind them, growled quietly with his hair rising on his haunches. There was such a stillness in the air: a feeling of expectancy, as if someone was watching and listening intently. They exhaled slowly, and the steam from their breath rose in the air. "It's weird how the air gets so cold, right?" Corbin said in a whisper.

They looked around the house. Everything looked the same as when they had left yesterday. They walked into her office and up to the typewriter. The bold capitalized letters of MURDER blazoned out at them. The keys on the typewriter trembled and shimmied slightly. "Did you see that?" Corbin said in a low voice.

"Yep, I sure did," Charlee whispered back. Suddenly, there was a scraping and thumping sound coming from above their heads. "I guess it's time to check out the attic," Charlee said reluctantly. Her face was white, and her brown eyes filled her face.

"Do you have a ladder?" Corbin asked.

"The realtor told me there was a ladder that folds down when you open it." She went to the hallway and pointed to a cord that was hanging down from the ceiling. She gave it a yank, and it didn't budge.

"Here, let me try." Corbin yanked on the cord twice and it gave, allowing him to pull the stairs down, unfolding as they went. "Do you have a flashlight?" Charlee nodded that she did and raced off to get it. She returned quickly and held it up to him. He was halfway up the ladder. He turned it on as he got to the last rung and shone it around the attic.

"What do you see up there?" Charlee called up to him.

"Well, not much. There are mousetraps laid out. Ew, looks like there are a few captives. They don't stink though. Must have been here a while. Ah, wait a minute. There's a wood crate or box—something like that. It must have been the sound you heard. I'm not sure how sturdy the floor is. I'm gonna see if I can stretch out and reach it," he said in a muffled voice. His feet disappeared into the attic. She heard a scraping, scratchy sound as he reached the box and pulled it to him.

"Please be careful, and don't fall through the ceiling. I don't think I could handle that right now, okay?"

"Yeah, I don't think I could either." His feet reappeared and stretched out to the top rung of the ladder. "It's not very heavy, and it's the only thing I saw up there, except for the traps." He carefully edged down the ladder, placing the box on the floor. Chewy sniffed it suspiciously. "Let's bring it over to the table and check it out." He hoisted it carefully and placed it on her table. He lifted the lid with a small squeak from its hinges, and they peered inside.

"There are pictures and newspaper articles in here. I think this is a box of mementos," Charlee said excitedly. "Wow! I think this is a military medal!" She held it up for Corbin to see.

"I think it's army. Or wait a minute, I think it's air force. Here's a picture of guys in uniforms in front of some planes," Corbin said with interest. "Can you make out their faces? Does one of them look like your ghost?"

Charlee stared intently at the picture. "No, it's too blurry. I can't tell. But look, here's their names listed. And wow! Look at this! Leopold Chaput! This is his box! Holy crap!" She continued to dig through the box. She pulled out a few newspaper clippings from the *Daily Courier*. "This is for an award in journalism, and oh my God, the journalist is Leopold Chaput! I don't think he's the murderer," she said reflectively. She pulled out a wedding picture in a glass frame. The young couple stared out at her with serious faces. "Wow! This must be him! It's a really old picture." She stared at their faces intently.

"I think this is the article you were talking about at the library," Corbin said, handing her the clipping. She smoothed it out the yellowed edges carefully. It was the article of the young couple that died in the car accident and the baby that went missing. "Looks like the baby was his granddaughter—so sad." A cupboard in the kitchen suddenly opened and shut. They jumped with a start and looked at each other. "Yep!" they said in unison nervously.

There were a number of other articles from the *Daily Courier* that had been written by Leopold Chaput. The last dated article was of the young couple and the car accident. "It seems like that's where it ended for Chaput. I wonder what happened? I wonder if the baby was ever found," Corbin thoughtfully mused aloud. The windowpanes rattled slightly in the kitchen. They both sat staring sadly at the box.

"I know what I'm gonna do tomorrow when I get to work," Corbin stated with determination.

"What?" Charlee said absently, deep in thought about the contents of the box.

"I'm going back to police files from 1950. I think Chaput was the guy that got murdered, and there's more to this story!" All the cupboards and drawers in the kitchen simultaneously opened and shut. Chewy began barking furiously. "For the love of God! Grab some of your stuff. You're coming back to my house!" he said authoritatively, looking around the room anxiously. "Well, I mean if you'd like to, that is." He smiled apologetically. "Didn't mean to sound so bossy. Let's get out of here."

Charlee laughed. "Okay." She rushed into her room, grabbed a duffel bag, threw in some jeans, a T-shirt, a nightgown, and went into the bathroom and grabbed her makeup bag. Heading into the kitchen, she got Chewy's dog food and biscuits. "I'm ready," she said a little breathlessly. Corbin was waiting for her at the already opened door. He had been watching her with admiration as she had whirled about the house.

They stepped out the door, and without touching it, it slammed shut behind them with a bang.

CHAPTER 30

Later in the day, they were sitting on Corbin's deck, basking in the rays of the cool December sun. Corbin had wrapped a blanket around her as the winter air was pretty chilly. They were both sipping a glass of wine with their feet up on the railing of the deck.

"I'm sure glad it's Sunday, and you didn't have to work today. This is so nice sitting out here. It's so pretty! If I was an artist, I would paint this view," she said, smiling at Corbin. She stretched her legs a little more and raised her face to be kissed by the sun. The tendrils around her face lifted with the breeze.

"I love how you take in the moment," he said with a contented voice as he sipped on his wine. Impulsively, he leaned over and gave her a quick kiss. "Sorry, I couldn't help myself, with you sitting there looking so pretty. You were daring me to kiss you, right?" he smiled mischievously.

"Well, yes! What took you so long?" she smiled with her dimples flashing. She leaned back with a sigh. "This is nice today after so much crazy. Such a sad family story with the baby missing and all. I wonder if the missing baby died and if that's the crying baby I've heard."

"Yeah, I think whatever we discover is going to be some pretty sad stuff." He looked at Charlee pensively. "Charlee, I don't want to pry, but you don't mention your family much. Are your parents aware of all this spooky stuff you're going through since you moved up here?" He gazed off into the distance, not looking at her directly.

Charlee hesitated before answering. "No, I haven't told them anything. They were completely against me moving up here. When I showed them the real-estate ad and picture of my house, they were very upset. My mother went to bed immediately with a sick head-ache, and my dad rushed for the whiskey bottle. It's weird because they were encouraging me to move on with my life but flipped out on the idea of Oregon."

"Maybe they didn't like the idea of their only daughter moving so far away? I'm sure they probably miss you a lot."

"One would think. I know they love me, but miss me? Not so sure. They always provided the best for me. We lived in a beautiful home on the lakeshore and had an amazing speedboat. I never lacked anything. I always felt like an outsider though—an intruder in their world. They only have eyes for each other. They live in their own beautiful bubble of champagne, Sinatra music, sunsets, and gourmet food. My dad would do anything for his queen. I don't really know why they had me. I was surely in the way…I'm rambling. I'm sorry I've said too much." She cut the conversation abruptly. Her dark eyes looked out over the vista and held the sadness of many lonely years. "Hey! I think your phone's ringing." As he got up to answer the phone, she thought to herself, *There I go again, I draw people close to me, and then I push them away.*

Corbin quickly strode to the sliding door, opened it, and grabbed the phone off the wall. "Hello? Wow! That's great! Yeah, yeah, okay. I'll tell her. Take it easy now. I'll see you soon. Bye." Corbin replaced the phone on the receiver. "That was Peggy. She's back home and going to be okay, and she's going into her shop for about an hour tomorrow. She has to go to the bank and stuff and wants you to come by about ten. She says she remembers something about the typewriter," he said to Charlee as he sat back down on his deck chair.

"Really? I wonder what it could be…so glad she's okay." She shivered as she pulled her blanket tightly around her, swallowing the contents of her wine.

CHAPTER 31

C harlee rushed into Peggy's shop the next morning at 10:00 a.m., swearing at the Santa, who mechanically greeted his *ho ho* welcome. "Peggy! Peggy! Where are you?" she called out.

"Hey! I'm coming. I'm coming! I could hear you cussing out my Santa from the back!" She laughed her throaty, raucous laugh. She threw her arms open, and Charlee ran to them to give her a big hug. "I'm okay, really I am. The doctor said it was merely an episode, whatever that is, right? I couldn't wait to get out of that stupid hospital and Nurse Ratchett," she said, her mischievous eyes twinkling. "Besides, we still have a ghost mystery to solve."

"Corbin said you remembered something about the typewriter? Here, let's go and sit down and get you off your feet."

"Okay, okay, but don't start babying me. I'm just fine! Well, it might not mean anything. It's just one little thing." She leaned across the table for her cigarettes, lighting one and inhaling deeply with satisfaction.

Charlee watched her with growing impatience. "For the love of God! What did you remember?" She smiled at Peggy, shaking her head but leaning forward for an answer.

Enjoying her torment, she took another long drag off her cigarette. "Well, the lady I bought it from that day, so many years ago now, said the typewriter had belonged to a newspaper journalist, probably the *Daily Courier* I'm thinking. See, I told you it wasn't much." She leaned backed in her chair, hitting on her cigarette again.

As she registered the information, Charlee blinked rapidly and said, "Wow! When you were in the hospital, the next day, Corbin and I went into my attic and found a box of old stuff from the owner, Leopold Chaput. There were newspaper clippings and awards, even a medal from the air force. There was a journalist award and articles that he wrote! He was a journalist! Holy crap! Could that mean that the typewriter belonged to him and that the ghost and the owner of my house are all connected to this guy Chaput?" She tossed her hair back over her shoulder and looked around the room, the enormity of this information sinking in. She stared at Peggy, dumbfounded.

The door banged open, and then a resounding *ho ho ho* from Santa. "Hey! Charlee! Peggy! Are you here?" It was Corbin. They both exhaled, happy it wasn't a customer in the middle of their revelation.

"Yeah, we're back here, Corbin," Charlee called out. As soon as Corbin appeared around the corner, Charlee relayed the news Peggy had given her about the typewriter.

"Wow! That's crazy! It seems like it could be his, right?" He shook his head in amazement. "I found out something at the police station." He paused. "Chaput was murdered by a blunt force to his head. In other words, his head was bashed in. Charlee, I'm sorry...I know this is shocking!" he said with concern and apologetically.

"We're finally getting somewhere. So to get this straight—I'm living in Leopold Chaput's house, who was murdered. His daughter and son-in-law died in a car crash. His granddaughter disappeared, and the crazy-ass, haunted typewriter probably belonged to him. How in the world did I get so lucky to be drawn into this crazy story?" She sat back in her chair and looked around the room with her large brown eyes wide.

"Yeah, no shit, right?" Peggy questioned with her cigarette dangling from her lips. "Now what?" Her fingers shook as she put her cigarette down.

"Charlee, walk me out, okay? I've got to get back to work."

"I'll be right back, Peggy," she said as she followed Corbin out the door.

"Charlee, there's something else I discovered in the files around that time. I didn't want to say in front of Peggy," he said seriously. Charlee looked at him with curious expectation. "You said before that your dad's name is Charles, right? What is your mom's name?"

"Her name is Marilyn. Why? What are you talking about?" Charlee stared up at him questioningly. She held her coat tightly around her, feeling the cold air chilling her to the bone.

"There may be a reason your parents didn't want you to move to Oregon. I found a file of a couple whose house burned down in Rogue River—suspected arson. It was never solved. The couple decided to move away. Their names were…Charles and Marilyn Wilkes. It said he was a Realtor and that they had a baby girl." He took a deep breath and looked at her. He had said all that pretty quickly. Her face was white with shock.

"But why? What the hell? Why in the world would they have not told me that we had lived up here? That I was born here? This doesn't make any sense. A fire? I've never heard any of this before! Are you sure you got the names right?"

He sadly nodded in the affirmative.

"They did react really strangely when I told them I was moving to Oregon. They've always been against it and didn't even want to talk about it. How weird and secretive! Why the mystery? Bad memories? But why not just tell me?" Anger began to flash in her dark eyes. "Well, I'm going to find out! I'm going to call them right now and see what this is all about?" She put her head through the door and called out to Peggy, "I'll see you later! Gotta go!"

Corbin looked at her with concern. "If you're going to call them, do it at my house, okay? Just in case at your house…" His voice trailed off. "Do you want to wait till I get off work?"

"Yeah, I'll go to your house. Chewy is still there too anyways. But no, go to work. I can do this on my own. I'll be okay. Really!" She smiled up at him weakly. She hopped into her Jeep and drove off, not looking back.

Such a strange story. I wonder what she'll find out. Why all the secrets—and arson too? Poor kid! I feel like there's a dark story here, and it's not gonna be pretty. Her Jeep disappeared out of his sight. He sighed and walked toward his patrol car. A few snowflakes drifted down from the cold white sky. A storm was coming.

CHAPTER 32

She dialed her parent's phone number—ringing and ringing. She felt shaky while holding the phone against her ear, almost dreading them to answer. It would probably be her dad that would answer. Her mother rarely went near the phone. With each ring, her resolve was diminishing. *Do I really want answers? Would things in my life shatter like crystal?* Still, she gripped the phone.

"Hello?" Her father's voice sounded so far away. At first, she didn't answer. She felt frozen. "Charlee, sweetie, is that you?" His voice was hesitant and waiting for her reply.

"Yeah, Dad, it's me. Sorry I haven't called for a while. I've been having a pretty strange time here. This is going to sound crazy, but it looks like I bought a haunted house." She went down the line in sequence regarding the weird supernatural occurrences she had experienced since moving there. Charles listened quietly, not interrupting. "So," she continued with difficulty, "I've made a few friends… they've been very helpful—the lady that sold me the crazy typewriter and a cop here in town." She finished breathlessly.

There was silence on the other line. She could hear him breathing. "Dad?"

"You're friends with a cop, you said?" His voice was quiet and measured. She strained to hear him.

"Yeah, and he told me something very strange, on top of the murdered guy named Chaput and his haunted typewriter." She took a deep breath and blurted it out. "He said you and mom lived here with me as a baby in Rogue River, and your house was burnt down by arson. No one was ever caught. What in the world is this about? You've never said anything about living in Oregon before!"

Charles sat heavily down in the chair beside his desk. His shoulders slumped. He closed his eyes, looking into the past. Their beautiful white two-story home was engulfed in flames while firemen rushed back and forth yelling commands—the devastation, all their possessions, his art collection, their history, everything. Not everything—he looked over at Marilyn, standing at the edges of their property in her long white satin dressing gown. *Pretty as a picture*, he thought. She was holding their baby, Charlee, in her arms tightly, gazing and transfixed at the fire blazing wildly in the background. She looked like a goddess before the gates of hell. She turned her head slowly and looked at him; an orange halo surrounded her white attire. Her eyes were wild and dark and not afraid—madness. She smiled charmingly and said, "Charles, darling, isn't it beautiful? And we're all okay," she smiled complacently and returned her fixation to the fire. The baby screamed in her arms. Marilyn was holding the baby nearly upside down and unaware of its distress. The terror in the baby's eyes matched his own.

"Dad...are you still there?" she asked quietly. The phone had been silent, but she could hear his light breathing.

"Charlee, I'll have to get back to you. Your mother is calling. She needs me..." His voice trailed off as he hung up the phone without saying goodbye.

"But...what about me?" Her voice was a whisper. She looked sadly at the phone held tightly in her hand. She hung it up quietly on the receiver. Same as it always was—she felt invisible.

CHAPTER 33

Charles went to their liquor cabinet and poured himself a double whiskey. He walked woodenly over to his black, baby grand piano and sat down. He touched the keys lightly, looking out the window at the lake in the distance. Abstractedly, he began to lightly play a tune. His dark brown eyes were sorrowful and his handsome face grave. He was still a good-looking man with graying temples rimming his dark hair. He had kept his body fit too. He gazed at the picture of Marilyn atop the piano. She was still so beautiful. The years had barely touched her—always elegant and graceful. Appearances were very important to him.

His mind traveled back in time and remembered the first time he had met her. She had taken his breath away. They were in Chicago. He was bringing real-estate papers for the hospital administrator at St. Luke's to sign. He was selling the administrator a beautiful, luxurious house that was not too far from Lake Michigan. She was sitting out-side on a bench in a garden that was between two of the buildings. St. Luke's was a Gothic-Renaissance architectural-style building—large, massive, and a little frightening. She looked like a princess that had stepped out of a fairy tale. She was sitting so quietly, so enraptured, and deep in thought. Her light blond hair lifted slightly in the breeze and caught the sunlight. She was wearing a long white dress with a blue velvet shawl around her shoulders. He approached her quietly and cautiously, afraid to startle her and have her disappear. She had a rather otherworldly look about her.

She heard him approach and turned her head to him. *Lovely!* With her pale alabaster skin, her sky-blue eyes, her silky blond hair, he was speechless. Her lips parted in a smile, exposing dazzling white teeth. Holding her hand out to him, she greeted him with an engaging smile. "I've been waiting for you," she said, in a voice as smooth and soft as satin, and patted the seat beside her.

He sat down and stared into her sparkling blue eyes. "For me?" His voice was a whisper. He was completely enchanted.

"Aren't you the new doctor my father was sending over to me?" Charles shook his head no. "Oh my goodness! I'm so sorry! I didn't mean to make you feel uncomfortable! I'm Marilyn." She tilted her head back and laughed. It was the most delightful sound he had ever heard.

The year was 1949, and since then, he was still enraptured and would do anything for her. Her laughter, touch, and everything about her was what he lived for. She was his world.

Her father had tried to discourage him from marrying her. Charles had discovered that she was staying at the hospital in the psychiatric wing due to a nervous breakdown. Her father, Lloyd, had confided to him that he frankly didn't know what to do with her. He admitted that she was very spoiled and had dangerous moods. Her mother had refused funding Marilyn another trip to Paris, and in the middle of the night, the father had caught Marilyn attempting to smother her mother with a pillow. After the attack, Marilyn went into a trancelike state, and her father had taken her to St. Luke's for a psychiatric evaluation. The mother was too frightened for her to return home.

Lloyd sadly agreed to their marriage if Charles would move far away with her. Perhaps a new beginning would be healing for her. He gave Charles a large dowry for her, and they quietly relocated to Oregon. Lloyd McCormick was of the wealthy and prominent McCormick family and was considered old money. As much as he loved his daughter, she had never wanted anything. He did not want any scandal in the paper about her mental state.

He continued playing the piano and drifted into "Moonlight Sonata," his favorite of Beethoven. This melody was always so moving to him and elevated his mood with its haunting and mysterious tone. Here he could lose himself in his music. In his soul, he knew the song would end.

Marilyn appeared in the doorway, smiling. Her long blond hair hung loosely to the side. "Charles, darling! You do play so beautifully! That is lovely! But you look so sad!" Her voice was soft and airy. She smiled again, her face not holding any expression of concern.

Unreachable, but she walks in beauty, he thought. "I'm never sad when you are in the room, my dear." Mentally, he pushed aside his conversation with Charlee and any worries of the future. *I'll come back to that later*, he thought. He pushed himself away from the piano. "Can I make you a drink? Or perhaps you're hungry now? It is nearly lunchtime." He walked with her to the dining room and held out a chair for her.

"Oh, you do spoil me so, Charles! And, of course, you know I love it!" Her smile lit up her pretty face, and tilting her head, she laughed. Charles rushed off to the kitchen to make lunch. Returning with a tray of sandwiches and salad, he stopped midstep when he saw Marilyn at the window, gazing out at the lake. Her eyes held that familiar, faraway look. She slowly turned her haunted eyes toward him. "There is a storm coming, isn't there, Charles?" Her words seemed laden with portent and hung in the air.

CHAPTER 34

When Corbin got home after work, he discovered Charlee sitting at his kitchen counter, staring out the window with a sad and inward expression. He had a feeling the conversation with her parents didn't go well. She turned to him and attempted a smile.

"Well, how'd it go? What did your parents say?" Corbin asked quietly.

"Actually, my dad didn't say anything. I told him everything. He listened. Then he said he had to go to my mother, and he hung up. He really didn't tell me anything." She pursed her lips and sighed. Thoughtfully she looked at him and said, "With that information you found about the arson, did you get an address?" she asked with interest.

"Yeah, I did…what are you thinking?" he said carefully, anticipating her response.

"I want to go and check out that property. I know it's cold and starting to snow, but it shouldn't take long, right?" She smiled, flashing her dimples.

"You are very hard to resist! You know that, right?" He smiled at her, shaking his head.

"But of course! Come on, Chewy. We're going for a ride!" They piled into Charlee's Jeep with Chewy covering the back seat and breathing dog breath heavily on them.

They found the address with little trouble. It was on Wards Creek Road, not far up from the cemetery. Before getting out of the car, Corbin took Charlee's hand and asked, "I don't know what you're hoping to find, but there may be nothing. This fire was a long time ago. Don't set your hopes too high, okay?"

"I know. I guess I'm just curious. It just all seems so strange." She got out of the car and scanned the area with searching eyes. Light snowflakes were falling. Chewy bounded out of the car, immediately lifted his leg on a bush, and went off exploring the property. "That looks like the remains of a chimney over there." She walked over to the forlorn stack of rocks—remaining emblems of a past where people had lived and sat in front of a fire. "I wonder what happened. And why did they never tell me? Why the secrets?" She kicked at a loose rock.

"I don't know, Charlee. Maybe the memory was too painful for them? Maybe when they moved, they just put Oregon behind them and didn't look back," Corbin said reflectively. He pulled his hood over his head to block out the falling snowflakes.

"Yeah, maybe." Chewy was running around the property, chasing a squirrel and barking happily. He came running back up to Charlee with something in his mouth and laid it at her feet. "I don't feel like playing stick right now, Chewy," she said with a little exasperation but bent down to pick it up and toss it anyway. "Wait, this isn't a stick. What is it?" She brought it up closer to examine it. "It looks like a metal baby rattle. It's pretty old and tarnished," she said excitedly. "Could this be my baby rattle—all that's left from the fire? Look, Corbin. What do you think?"

Corbin took it from her hands, brushing off the dirt and snow and then rubbing it against his jacket. "Charlee, there's something written on it." He spit on it and rubbed it a little harder. "There's three letters here: CEW. Wow! This could be your baby rattle, and there's your initials!" He held it out to her so she could closely examine it.

She turned it over in her hands and stared at the initials—CEW. "Yeah, those look like initials. But what's really strange, Corbin, is… my initials are CAW: Charlee Ann Wilkes." They both looked at each other puzzled. This was disturbing. What did it mean? The snow was starting to come down a little harder. Charlee's gaze wandered around the barren property. "Come on. Let's get out of here." They walked slowly back to the Jeep, Chewy bounding behind them. As she was getting in her car, she looked over her shoulder sadly at the desolate fireplace chimney being covered with snow. Soon, it would be obliterated from view.

CHAPTER 35

After a few days of lounging around Corbin's house and pushing the world away, it was time to move forward and do something. She hadn't heard back from her father, and she wasn't surprised. It was very typical.

She looked out the window at the falling snow—such a quiet world. Everything seemed so peaceful and asleep under the deepening white blanket. *I have to come to grips with this*, she thought. *I have to go home. I can't keep hiding away here at Corbin's house. Although, it's been really nice. Corbin was very attentive and a wonderful cook. He sings and plays his guitar beautifully too.* She sighed. *I should call my dad again too and not let him off the hook. He owes me some answers. I really need to face this ghost thing and decide what to do about it. Should I move? Would it follow me?* The bashed-in, pulsating gore of the man with the sunken eyes flashed in her memory. She shuddered at the horror. *Maybe there's something more in that box of mementos that I missed.* She looked at the battered baby rattle lying on the countertop. The initials CEW were disturbing. What did it mean? Her initials were CAW, and her dad's were CSW for Charles Stephen Wilkes—very weird.

Her attention was drawn outside again, watching Chewy running around happily in the backyard. He was leaping and digging his big nose into the snow. *He's such a big puppy sometimes*, she thought, laughing to herself. *I sure love that horse of a dog! I'm glad he's been happy here at Corbin's. This whole haunted house thing hasn't been easy on him either. He's been so protective.* As if he knew she was thinking about him, he stopped his romping and looked up at her, his eyes locking on hers. She smiled and waved at him. He continued his prancing in the snow. *Ha! I feel sorry for Corbin when the snow melts and he discovers all the doggy landmines Chewy has left him.*

She picked up the rattle, frowning and turning it over and over in her hands.

*****

Charles was staring out his window too. The lake was so beautiful bordered by the snowbanks. Normally, he loved the Christmas season. He had already set up their tree, with the lights and decorations; and Marilyn had laughed and clapped her hands in delight, as if she was a child. The tree sat sparkling with tiny lights in the corner, evoking thoughts of excitement and Christmas magic. *Such incongruity*, he thought sadly as he pulled his typewriter closer to him on his desk.

He pulled open his desk drawer and pulled out several sheets of paper. He slowly placed a sheet in his typewriter. This was the moment, a day in time, that he had dreaded for many years. He reached for his tumbler of whiskey and took a long sip, savoring the taste of the Crown Royal before he let it slide down his throat. He had always appreciated the finer things in life—a beautiful home, expensive luxury cars, designer clothes, speedboats, and a gorgeous wife. He sighed deeply: he knew it wouldn't last forever. He knew what he had to do, however reluctantly.

His hands trembled as they hovered over the keys. He began to type. "Dearest Charlee…" He gasped and held on to the side of the desk as the horrible, hideous memory that he had pushed aside for so many years smashed into his memory. He could no longer close out that horrible vision: the scream, the sound of heavy metal crunching through bone, and the blood. God, there was so much blood. He watched the light fade from the serious, sad brown eyes, and then there was silence, except for his own ragged breathing. And then he ran, slamming the door behind him with his pulse rushing in his ears. Guilt followed him.

He continued typing.

CHAPTER 36

A nother few days had passed of ignoring the task at hand. She knew she had to confront her issues with her dad and at her house. But she had chosen happily to decorate Corbin's house for Christmas and to bake gingerbread and Christmas cookies.

When Corbin walked in the door after work, he saw her determined face and asked, "So you're ready to face this now?"

She nodded quickly.

"Okay, let me go and change my clothes." Within minutes, he had returned and found her already in her coat and Chewy on his leash. "Okay, let's do it!"

They drove slowly to her house, sliding a little on the ice going down the steep slope of Broadway. It was nearly dark when they arrived in front of her house. As they walked up the pathway to her house, all the lights in the house turned on. She could feel Chewy stiffen beside her. As they approached the door, it opened with a squeak. They looked at each other and nodded, stepping into the doorway. Charlee bent down and scooped up the mail that had been pushed through the slot. It was several days' worth of mail, so it was quite a bundle. She walked slowly into the kitchen and placed it on the table. The memento box was still on the table.

The blender suddenly turned on, followed by the stereo, and then the TV. The stereo and TV were on full blast—deafening and chaotic. The music from the stereo was the same song that had blasted before, "You Are My Sunshine." The air was alive with static electricity. Every hair on her arms were standing up. Corbin rushed over to the TV and turned it off, and Charlee ran to the stereo. They both turned on again.

"Unplug everything," Corbin yelled over the noise. Charlee unplugged the stereo and ran over and unplugged the blender too. Corbin yanked on the TV plug. "He sure isn't wasting much time, is he?" he said, his breath coming in steamy gasps. The temperature had plunged, and their breath was seen in the air.

"As if it isn't cold enough already," Charlee managed to squeak out. Chewy was growling lowly, and his hair was raised on his haunches. Frost had developed on the windows and was quickly developing icy patterns across the panes. Charlee's heart was pounding in her chest. *This is crazy*, she thought madly.

A fire suddenly blazed in the fireplace, crackling and popping. "That isn't possible!" Charlee gasped out. "The fireplace doesn't even work. It's boarded up. Hasn't worked in years the realtor said." They both stared in amazement at the blazing fire. Cupboard doors began opening and slamming shut. The noise was unnerving.

A sound of clacking typewriter keys began in her office. Their eyes were open wide with fear. The entire house began to tremble and then shake as if in a low Richter scale earthquake. Chewy barked loudly in fear. The whispery voice began, first low in intensity and then gaining in volume: "I HAVE THE STORY!" It repeated and repeated. They held their hands over their ears. Chewy howled in terror. A wind began to circle throughout the room, blowing the curtains up in the air and the newspapers off her coffee table. The wind became stronger. They clasped hands and began to walk to her office. They were bent against the wind and held on to the doorways as they went.

"Holy shit! I can't believe this!" Charlee screamed out. Seated at her desk was the shimmery form of Leopold Chaput. He was translucent. They could see knotty pine on the wall behind him. His hands were poised on the keys before him, and he was typing furiously.

Corbin choked out, "This is unbelievable!" They both held on tightly to Chewy, who was trying to lunge ahead. The curtains billowed wildly. As they drew a little closer, they could see the spirit's bashed in skull. The gore of his remaining brains glistened and pulsed. His form seemed to shimmer and dim, becoming less visible until all you could see were his ghostly hands typing rapidly at the typewriter. Corbin squinted and moved a little closer, with Charlee lagging behind. He wanted to see what was being typed.

"What is it? What's he typing?" Charlee forced her voice to speak out loud. She barely recognized her hoarse voice.

"It's all blended together in capital letters. Let me see." He focused his eyes and moved in a little closer, forcing himself against the wind. "It says CWLETTERCWLETTERCWLETTER. Keeps repeating that over and over. What could that mean?"

The spectral hands continued to type fiercely. To their horror, blood suddenly began to pore from the typewriter onto the ghostly hands. The blood poured out in pulsing gushes as if from a water pump. It dripped down from the spectral hands onto the typewriter and cascaded to the floor. The pool of blood began to spread out and move toward them. Charlee began to scream, and Chewy was barking in terror. Corbin swiftly lifted Charlee up into his arms and backed out of the room, slipping on the blood and nearly falling on his way out the door. A baby's wailing cry pierced the air. Charlee buried her head in Corbin's shoulder, trying to block out the terrifying and haunting cry. Chewy was out the door ahead of them, banging into the walls.

The fire was still blazing in the fireplace, and the tempestuous wind was still swirling around the room. They could still hear the clacking of the keys in the next room.

"What could that mean? What is he typing?" Charlee screamed out over the cacophony of deafening sounds.

Corbin was shaking his head in shock. He blinked quickly, forming an idea in his mind. "Charlee, CW is your initials, right?" he yelled out.

"Yes, and so?" She looked at him with confusion.

"It kept saying *letter* after CW." The fire went out in the fireplace. They both stared at the fireplace, now cold and dark as if it had never been lit. "Charlee, maybe *letter* means mail." They looked over at the table where Charlee had tossed her mail when they entered. Suddenly, the stack of mail seemed ominous and foreboding.

Charlee mouthed the word *what* silently. The wind stopped. The curtains ceased billowing wildly about. The crying of the baby was hushed. She moved slowly toward the table. The typewriter silenced in the next room. The house became still; and there was an air of expectancy, as if the spirit of Leopold Chaput was listening with hypervigilance.

The air remained frigid. Charlee, with cold numb fingers, rifled through her mail. Corbin had his hand firmly planted on her shoulder, and Chewy was nudged between them. "Okay, there's junk mail, my power bill, credit card bill, another mailer, and a letter from my dad."

They both looked at the letter. In the top left margin of the envelope was printed CW for Charles Wilkes. She looked quickly into Corbin's eyes, mirroring his surprise. "This has something to do with my dad!" she exclaimed. "I don't get it! How could that be?" she asked in wonderment.

"I have no idea, Charlee, but I think you better read it!" Corbin said seriously. They both stared at the letter.

"Will you read it with me?" Charlee questioned, her voice trembling. She felt like she was plummeting down a slope out of control on a precipice of discovery—a mystery maybe she didn't want solved. She felt a little dizzy and pushed her hair away from her face, trying to steady herself.

Corbin noticed her swaying motion. "Of course, I will, sweetie." He pulled up the chairs, and they both sat down. She handed him the envelope to open. With shaky hands, he broke open the seal and slid the letter out. They both looked at each other and took a deep breath.

"Go ahead. Read it aloud. I just can't do it myself right now."

Corbin nodded. The house was dead silent. The only sound was Chewy's heavy breathing. He seemed to wait in anticipation too.

He opened the letter, smoothing it out in his hands.

"Dearest Charlee...," it began.

CHAPTER 37

Corbin continued reading after nervously clearing his throat:

Dearest Charlee,

I knew this day would come. I have dreaded it all your life. It is with great shame and a heavy heart that I have to confess to you that I am a fraud and have cheated you of your rightful heritage. You are going to be very shocked when you read what I am going to tell you. I hope someday you may find it in your heart to forgive me, but I will understand if you do not.

It grieves me to say that I am not your real father, and Marilyn is not your real mother. I know this is shocking news, and I can only hope you have friends around you for support when you read this letter.

I met Marilyn many years ago in Chicago. She was a patient in a mental wing at the hospital. She had some serious psychological issues. But I was in love, and I married her in spite of that. We moved away to Oregon at her father's request.

One night many years ago on the Fourth of July, we were driving down a winding road in Rogue River. Yes, you were born in Oregon. I had been drinking pretty heavily at a party we had attended. I was admiring Marilyn's beautiful face and did not notice the oncoming car. We swerved; but it forced the other car off the road, hitting a tree. The young couple inside were dead. There was a four-month-old baby in the back seat—a baby girl. Marilyn so desperately wanted a baby girl. You know I've never been able to tell her *no*. We took the baby for our own. You were that baby, Charlee.

You took the place of our baby boy that had recently died. His name was Charles Edward Wilkes. I am so horrified to have to tell you this, and I know you will think us monsters. I can't blame you for that. Charles was a colicky baby boy, and Marilyn had wanted a girl. He cried a lot at night. One night when he was crying, and I was fast asleep, Marilyn smothered him with a pillow to silence him. She had tried to kill her mother too in Chicago in the same fashion, which is why her father had us move. I was devastated and terrified with what she did to Charles. I took our precious little three-month-old baby boy to the nearby cemetery. There was a baby's grave there with an angel statue. I still remember the name on the marker: Anna Marie. I buried our baby on the top of the grave a few feet down and covered it with dirt and rocks. It was an undetectable and old neglected grave. I am so sorry to tell you these gruesome things of someone you trusted and called *dad*.

I'm afraid it gets worse. The grandfather of this baby girl was a journalist, and he was heartbroken with the loss of his daughter, son-in-law, and missing granddaughter. He saw Marilyn and I at an event in town, and he recognized you. He did his research and figured it out. He confronted me with it and told me to meet him at his house and that he had proof. I was so fearful of our arrest. I'm ashamed to say that I am a coward.

I went to his house, and we argued. I denied everything. When he turned his back on me to get his proof, I picked up his heavy typewriter and struck him a horrible blow to his head. There was so much blood! In absolute panic, I turned and ran. I left the poor man dying on the floor.

I never told Marilyn what I did. It was my dark secret. Not long after that, maybe a few days, I can't remember, Marilyn set the curtains on fire in the living room with a candle. She didn't know why she did it. She thought the flames were beautiful. It was difficult at times to cover for her madness. She had many spells of insanity, and that's why I would keep her in her room so often, telling you she had a migraine headache. Our beautiful home was burnt to the ground, and I realized it was time to move away before we were discovered for our crimes. I am so sorry, Charlee, that you are discovering that your entire life has been based on our lies.

To this day, I love Marilyn with my whole heart, and I cannot bear the thought of her being imprisoned in a mental institution or of me going to prison. She just wouldn't understand. She is so fragile.

I had hoped the past would never resurface, but with your innate desire to move to Rogue River and the supernatural occurrences in the very house of Leopold Chaput, I knew the end was near. Justice found its way.

The property in Rogue River is still in my name. You may have it, of course, along with our house and all our property in Lake Arrowhead.

My lawyer has a full list of all my assets. I know riches haven't meant as much to you as they have to me, but I want you to know you will be very wealthy.

All these years, you have been the best daughter anyone could ever imagine having, and I have loved you. I know right now that's pretty hard to believe. I want you to show this letter to your cop friend; he'll know what to do with it. I'm so deeply sorry. By the time you have read this letter, I will have taken mine and Marilyn's lives. It's the only way. I don't see any other solution; and the coward that I am, I cannot bear to see the shock and horror in your eyes knowing the truth about us.

I have one honest and decent thing I can return to you that is rightfully yours, which is your name: Aimee Elizabeth Deveraux.

Sincerely,
Charles Wilkes

Corbin folded the letter quietly and looked into Charlee's stricken face, which was devoid of color. He got up and poured a glass of brandy and held it to her lips. She took a few sips before her body was wracked with gut-wrenching sobs. She cried as a lost child in search of her missing parents.

CHAPTER 38

The fire was blazing brightly in the large stone fireplace. The lingering smell of the roast beef they had for dinner hung in the air. The twinkling lights on the Christmas tree sparkled in many colors and lit up the crystal ornaments. Colorful presents surrounded the bottom of the tree. The scented candles illumined the room in warm accents. Light Christmas music played on the stereo in the background. It was all so lovely. *Perfection*, Charles thought.

Lovely Marilyn sat on the couch, gazing complacently into the fire. The light from the fire lit up her platinum hair in a shiny halo. *She's still as beautiful as Carole Lombard*, Charles mused lovingly. She was dressed in a long white satin robe and a matching nightgown. Diamond earrings sparkled beneath the tresses of her blond tendrils. She lifted her crystal glass of Dom Perignon champagne to her full and rosy lips. She took a sip and smiled at Charles. "I do love Christmas so, Charles! It's all so beautiful! Magical, isn't it?"

Charles nodded.

"It reminds me of Christmas as a little girl. I'm afraid I was terribly spoiled!" she laughed with delight. "I think this Christmas will be very special! I can't wait to see what surprises you have for me this year!" She smiled with a teasing lilt in her voice. She reached out to the Santa platter on the coffee table and popped a rum-ball cookie into her mouth that Charles had made that morning. She savored it as it melted on her tongue. Charles had many talents—cooking, baking, and loving her.

She'd always been a vision of loveliness and so childlike. She hadn't mentioned Charlee's name since Charlee had moved to Oregon. He had brought up her name a number of times, but

Marilyn always changed the subject back to herself. When he had told her of her parents' death in a plane crash, she had said, "How sad!" With the news of all the money she would inherit, she said, "We should buy a bigger boat." And they did—out of sight and out of mind. He marveled at the lack of reflection. She never displayed any signs of regret, empathy, shame, or sorrow.

He looked down into his glass of champagne. The tiny golden bubbles rose to the surface. She was like a beautiful bubble, existing to be admired, enjoyed, and adored. He had been that willing bene-factor. If he had the choice, he would do it again. He was hopelessly enchanted with her charm and beauty. Sadly, he knew that others wouldn't feel that way. Harsh authorities would take her away from him and lock her up. And he would go to prison, unable to visit her and supervise treatment. That could not be allowed to happen. His dark eyes looked around the room sadly. For him, it was very hard to let go of a life that he dearly loved. He loved Marilyn, and he also loved all his expensive possessions that he had acquired over the years.

He sipped more champagne and stared into the warm crackling fire. It had stopped snowing, and that was a good thing. He stood up and walked over to the window. It was a quiet and blanketed world out there. Christmas lights twinkled from their home and the sur-rounding houses as well. The dark lake glimmered in the distance. Lights reflected off the dark surface. A lovely full moon hung in that impervious sky. Distant stars lit the sky. *It's a beautiful night*, Charles thought.

He turned and fingered the keys on his piano. "Oh, do play a Christmas song, Charles. Play "Oh Holy Night"! I love that one!" She joined him at the piano and began singing in a high sweet voice. *She even sings like an angel*, he thought.

At the finish of the song, Charles looked up at her, smiling, and said, "Tonight is a beautiful and magical night! Let's do something spontaneous and different!"

With a sudden sparkle in her eyes, Marilyn said a little breath-lessly, "What did you have in mind?" She loved the sound of adventure.

"I thought we'd pack up some champagne and treats and take a boat ride around the lake. We could see all the Christmas lights around the shore. I know it's cold out, but I will make sure you are bundled up in blankets. Doesn't that sound romantic?" He looked at her questioningly and then turned his eyes to look out the large picture window.

"What a lovely idea! I would love to see all the lights too! Should I change my clothes?"

"No, just put on your boots. I love seeing you in that white satin gown. Let me just throw a few things in a duffel bag to bring down to the boat," he said, leaving the room. He returned shortly with the supplies and a few blankets. He wrapped the blanket from the couch around her shoulders. "Ready?" He handed her a red rose from the vase on their way out the door.

They walked down the lit pathway to the boat. The night was still, and the stars twinkled in the dark sky. Marilyn began singing a tune that she had loved as a child. She would often sing it when she was happy. "You are my sunshine, my only sunshine. You make me happy when skies are gray. You'll never know dear how much I love you, so please don't take my sunshine away." She smiled brightly at Charles. He turned his head away so that she could not see the sudden tears that welled in his dark eyes.

When they reached the dock, Charles put the duffel bag down beside the boat and took Marilyn in his arms. He began to spin her in a waltz, and she gracefully twirled in his arms. The dance ended with him dipping her in a smooth movement, kissing her gently on the lips. "You dance divinely, Charles!" she giggled.

He guided her footing into the boat. It was a beautiful Viking luxury sport cruiser. The name on the side of the boat was *Marilyn*. He loved his boat. It was a treasured possession. He tucked an additional blanket around her shoulders and pulled the champagne out of the bag. He poured them both a glass and brought out a small crystal bowl of caviar. He went and turned on the motor to warm up the engine. When he returned to her, he clinked her glass in a toast and said, "Marilyn, I will love you to the end of our days. I would protect you with my life. You have always been my everything. You know that, right?" He was caressing her hair and looking deeply into her eyes.

"Charles, you sound so serious! I know that you love me! The feeling is mutual silly!" she said flirtatiously, laughing. "Let's talk about all the beautiful lights!" she exclaimed, waving her arms and encompassing the panoramic starlit sky and twinkling houses behind the luminous white snowbanks.

"Well, hold on. Let me drive us out onto the lake," he said laughing. He sat in the captain's chair and put the boat in gear. He drove around the north shore of the lake and over to edge of the docks by Lake Arrowhead Village. The village was charming, and its buildings were all in the Tudor style. It had been a favorite of Hollywood stars in the 1920s. The lights were dazzling. He drove back out to the middle of the lake, the deepest area, and stopped, turning off the engine.

He returned to his seat next to her. "And yes, you're right. It is an amazing sight!" He looked out at the expanse of sky and put his arm around her, holding her close and taking in the beauty of the night. A shooting star flung itself across the sky, followed by another star in close pursuit. "I would be that following star behind you, my love," Charles said, trying to mask the melancholy in his voice. Arms around each other with a light breeze lifting their hair, they lived in the moment.

"We should probably head back soon, Charles. It is really quite chilly."

"Let's have one more glass of champagne before we go. I want to savor the moment."

"Okay, I'm easy to talk into that! You know I've always loved champagne!" She handed him her glass. He turned away from her and went to the little cooler he had in the duffel bag. He filled their glasses and resolutely dropped the potent contents of the Nembutal pills into her glass. He watched the powder swirl with the bubbles of champagne. *A little toxic waltz*, he thought. "Concentrate. Do not hesitate," he told himself. He sat beside her, linking his arm in hers, and said, "Marilyn, I love you so much! Till death do us part." He drank, sipping slowly and watching her carefully. After several minutes, she drained her glass and in a dramatic voice said, "Now, take me home, Charles, before I catch my death of cold."

"Okay, let me just reorganize and straighten up here." He picked up their glasses and put them in the bag. He picked up the half-full bowl of caviar. "I think I'll give the fish a treat." Taking his time, he dumped the contents into the water, staring into the swirling depth. He looked over at Marilyn, and she was blinking and shaking her head.

"Charles, I suddenly feel funny, really tired, but very weird… I…I…" She leaned back and was in a prone position. Her head was tilted back, with her eyes closed and her mouth slightly open. He put his head down on her heart, and the beating was barely perceptible. The drug had worked. He pulled the blanket away from her. *She's so beautiful in the moonlight in her white satin*, he thought stifling a sob. He held her hand, bringing it to his lips, and kissed it. He could smell her Chanel perfume on her wrist. "I'm so sorry. It was the only way!" he choked out hoarsely. He laid his head on her chest and cried. He let it go and wailed. The tears were streaming down his face, and his cries echoed in the darkness.

When he was spent, he had no tears left. He pulled himself up, went to where the anchor was stored, and unbolted it from the boat. He took the three pieces of rope from the duffel bag. He tied one length firmly around Marilyn's ankle and the other around his. He tied the last rope around her wrist, and with the other end, he would bind his wrist at the last moment. He fastened the ropes around their ankles to the anchor. He knew what to do. He had been planning this since Charlee moved to Oregon. He had intuitively known the end was near. He gently lifted the red rose, inhaling its sweet fragrance—a symbol of their love—and tossed it into the dark water.

He hoisted the anchor to the side of the boat so he could just slide it into the water. Removing a small flask from his pocket, he drained the contents in a long gulp. He gently lifted Marilyn into his arms, binding their wrists together. He sat on the edge of the boat, holding her in his arms and cradling her. Looking at her lovingly, he pushed the anchor into the water. They were both pulled into the water, barely making a splash.

The water was frigid. "Don't fight it," he told himself. He looked above to the starry sky. They began sinking slowly. He drew Marilyn close to him, his arms around her. Their descent was in a slow spiral. Air escaped from their lungs and rose above them in small bubbles. *It's like champagne bubbles*, he thought with wonder. Marilyn was still so beautiful, even in death. Her white satin gown fanned out gracefully. Her blond hair swirled about her face, weightless. The pressure of the water forced Marilyn's eyes open. Looking into her eyes, he held her in a tighter embrace. Continuing in their sinuous spiral downward, Charles thought with satisfaction, *It's our last waltz—our death waltz.*

CHAPTER 39

Corbin held her until her tears stopped. He gave her a paper towel to dry her face, and he picked up the letter and said, "He says I would know what to do with this. I do. You know what it is, don't you?" he said to her in a very somber tone.

"Yes, I do. You have to take it to the police station and report this. It's so hard to believe," she said in a trembling whisper. "They were never my parents! He killed my grandfather, and both my parents died because of him. And she killed her own son! My life is a lie! I can't even say *mom* or *dad* because they never were! And now they're dead too! Oh my God!" Tears were welling up in her eyes again. "That beautiful couple in the paper were my parents! Wow!" Her tears spilled down her face. "This is so much to take in. I'm all alone. I don't have a family." Her voice ended in the faintest of whispers.

Corbin took her hands and stared into her devastated face. "I know it's a lot to take in—it's horrendous. But you are not alone. You have me and Peggy, and we will help you get through this. You will get through this. You are very strong and are a survivor." Snow slapped up against the windowpanes in front of them with a stinging sound. The house was silent, and they could hear the wall clock ticking.

Charlee picked up the article out of the box with her smiling parents. "They look nice, don't they? I guess Leopold Chaput must have really loved them and me to get me all the way up here, scare me to death, and have the truth exposed finally. I guess he's a pretty strong spirit."

"It's very touching, in a scary sort of way," Corbin said with a wry smile.

Charlee smiled back and then said, "The baby's cry that we've heard must be that of the baby boy that she killed. How could she do that? She must have been really sick! It's amazing that I didn't see that. I always just thought she was a little dramatic and had migraine headaches. It actually explains a lot in my life now, how I always felt like an outsider. I was." She looked sadly at the smiling couple.

Chewy rose up from the floor with a grunt and placed his large head into her lap. He looked sorrowfully at her with his large bloodshot eyes. He whined and wagged his tail. Corbin laughed and said, "He sure is expressive, right?" He patted Chewy's head. "Okay, Chewy, let's go back to my house, and we'll report all this stuff tomorrow to my office. There's nobody there right now. Is that good with you?" he questioned Charlee.

"Yeah, let's get out of here." She grabbed the letter and the article of her parents and put them in her purse. After opening the front door, they looked at the rapidly falling snow. "Wow! It's really been coming down! You can barely see our footprints. It's a good thing I have a four-wheel drive." There were no cars on the road. They drove slowly up the steep hill of Broadway, not talking and deep in thought.

There was a large cross lit up in the sky behind Corbin's house. "The neighbors light it every year," Corbin explained—a sign of hope. They pulled into Corbin's driveway. His house looked so welcoming with all the twinkling Christmas lights bordering his windows and roof. Corbin squeezed Charlee's hand.

The next morning, they walked into the police station. Charlee brought out the letter and explained the entire story, starting from her inclination to move to Oregon. The chief of police listened quietly, holding the letter in his hands and looking at the article. "I remember my dad telling me about this story. It was very tragic. There was a search for the baby. Looks like it was you. The grandfather was devastated and refused to give up. And then the grandfather, Leopold Chaput, was dead—so heartbreaking. Apparently, the mystery is finally being solved." He pulled at his moustache thoughtfully. "As far as your spiritual references, I would rather not add this in my notes. I don't want this to not be taken seriously, not meaning any disrespect. You understand?" He looked at Charlee sympathetically. Charlee nodded in the affirmative.

"I will personally make calls to the Lake Arrowhead Police, and I'll get my men over to Woodville Cemetery. There is peace in closure." He got up and patted Charlee on the shoulder and said, "Corbin, I want you and Billy to go check out the cemetery right away, okay?"

"Will do! I'm just going to drive her home, and then I'm on it."

Corbin drove Charlee back to his house. "As soon as I have any news, I'll call you right away. I know it's tough, but try to relax. Drink my brandy. Eat all my ice cream. Whatever, okay?"

"I'm okay. I might take you up on that ice cream." She waved as he drove off.

*****

Corbin watched Billy, his partner, dig on the grave under the tomb stone of Anna Marie. After digging carefully a few feet down, Billy exclaimed, "Oh boy, here we go. We've got something." He got down on his knees and gingerly swept away the dirt exposing a tiny little skeleton wrapped in the remains of a blanket. "Oh my God!" Billy stood up quickly and walked away, overcome with emotion. He had two small children of his own.

Corbin stood there silently, staring at the small skeleton. He felt a deep sadness settling on him like a blanket of snow on his heart. *The poor baby! Finally, your tragedy is known and no longer a secret.* He looked at the inscription on the tombstone. Little Anna Marie had been loved and deeply missed. The injustice made the bile rise in his throat, and he choked back a sob. The cemetery was covered in snow, white and pristine and so quiet. There was no chatter of birds, and no cars drove by. Nature seemed to be in silent reverence to this tiny life that no one had noticed when he ceased to exist. Tears rolled down his cheeks, unobserved.

*****

As soon as Charlee got the call, she raced down to the police station. Corbin was waiting for her in the chief's office. He told her of the little skeleton they had discovered in the spot that Charles had told them to look.

"That is so heartbreaking," Charlee said sadly. "I will make sure he has a proper burial. Is there other news?"

Overhearing her as he walked in, the chief said, "Yes, there is. I got through to the Lake Arrowhead Police. The neighbors of Charles Wilkes reported that the couple had not returned with their boat from the night before. They could see it drifting on the lake with their binoculars. It didn't seem right to them, and they couldn't see anyone on the boat." He looked at Charlee's serious face and continued, "The boat patrol went out and discovered no one on board. They said it looked like they had been celebrating. There were empty bottles of champagne and a bowl with some remaining caviar. They said there was a red rose floating in the near proximity of the boat. There hasn't been much wind, so they don't think the boat drifted very much. It was in the deepest part of the lake, about a 185-foot depth, so divers won't go that deep because of getting the bends. Do you understand what the bends are?" he questioned Charlee.

"Yes, it's because of the water pressure and depth. There are horrible side effects from swimming to the surface too quickly."

"Right. So the police have decided to let them remain, especially given the evidence of your letter of an intentional suicide. I'm very sorry to have to tell you all of this," he said, meeting her eyes, sadly.

"The police made the right decision. He planned it all, obviously. He chose the deepest part of the lake so that no one would retrieve them. The champagne, caviar, red rose—he always did everything with an elegant flair. It stands to reason that he would do that with their deaths as well," she spoke quietly, without emotion in her voice. She was exhausted.

"I know you've been through an enormous ordeal. I had to notify the press of this news due to it being the closure of a murder and missing person case. A reporter from the *Daily Courier* is here and would like to ask you a few questions. Are you up to it?"

"Yes, I am. Corbin, would you come with me?"

"Of course, I will." He stood up and followed her out of the office. The reporter was very polite and only asked a few questions. He had most of the story from the chief.

When the interview concluded, Charlee said, "Corbin, I'm going home to call the mortuary and my...Charles's lawyer. I think I'll drop by and see Peggy first." She walked out the door and straightened her shoulders with her head held high.

Corbin watched her go and thought, *That is one special lady.*

Charlee walked into Peggy's shop, and the Santa greeted her with its *ho ho ho.*

"Shut up, Santa! Peggy, are you here?" She rounded the corner, nearly bumping into Peggy.

Peggy put out her arms and said, "Corbin told me everything!" Charlee put her head on Peggy's shoulder and gratefully accepted the hug. "Come on and sit down. I've been waiting for you. I have chocolate doughnuts and coffee." Charlee pushed her hair back from her face and laughed. "You do know how to reach me!" Outside, large snowflakes began falling again from a quiet gray sky.

CHAPTER 40

Chewy stretched his bulky frame in front of the warm crackling fire. He sighed deeply with satisfaction. It was so nice to be home again, and she was so happy with having her fireplace fixed and operating. It made the room look so much more cheerful and homey. Corbin had helped her get a tree and put lights up outside. She had bought some lights for the tree and some ornaments too. She stretched her feet in front of the fire and wiggled her toes. There had been no spectral visits, and she was content.

So much had happened in the past week. I'm so glad I bought the plot and headstone for the poor baby, she thought. It was a beautiful upright headstone with Jesus holding a baby. She had his name, Charles Edward Wilkes, engraved on it and when he was born. She had called State Records for his birth date but didn't know the date he died, so she guessed a month and left it at that. It was very pretty though. Corbin and Peggy had gone with her to the gravesite, with flowers, to say a prayer. They had been the only ones in the cemetery.

She felt lucky that she was able to buy the plot next to baby Anna Marie's grave. That seemed right somehow. They held hands, and Peggy said a prayer about babies, heaven, and being in the arms of God.

"Finally, little baby Charles has peace and will not be forgotten," Corbin said seriously. They all sadly nodded. Charlee leaned down and put an arrangement of red Christmas flowers in the vase on the headstone.

"Merry Christmas in heaven. Be at peace," she whispered.

*****

She took a sip off her glass of wine and leaned back comfortably. *It's going to seem strange not to have to worry about money anymore.* She had talked to Charles's lawyer, and she was now a wealthy woman. The house and everything in Lake Arrowhead was to be sold, including the boat. *Especially the boat.* She grimaced. The property at the ruins of the burned house was to be sold as well. She wasn't going to rush into anything and spend a lot of money. Taking her time sounded like a wise idea. *I'm going to keep my grandfather's little haunted house though,* she thought with a smile.

Her little Christmas tree sparkled with colored lights and ornaments. She had also made gingerbread men and hung them on the tree with red ribbons. Most of the cookies at the base of the tree were now missing legs and arms that Chewy had bitten off. She stared at the little maimed cookies, shaking her head with a laugh.

She hoped Corbin would like the present she bought him. It was a beautiful guitar case with his initials on the top. *It was wonderful hearing him play and sing. So much talent! It's awkwardly wrapped, but that's okay,* she thought with a smile.

They would be here soon, and she was a little nervous. Corbin and his father were coming to take her out for a Christmas Eve dinner. She went to the bathroom and looked at herself in the mirror. She was wearing a red angora sweater that dipped over her shoulder, jeans, and black leather boots. She had braided her long hair to the side and had pulled a few tendrils of hair out, framing her face. Her eyes sparkled with excitement. *I feel pretty tonight,* she thought happily.

The doorbell rang. *Wow! It works!* She had never heard it ring before. Chewy barked excitedly. She swung open the door. Corbin was standing there with an attractive older man in his fifties. He looked like an older version of Corbin—twinkling blue eyes and curly hair. "Merry Christmas!" they said in unison.

"Merry Christmas! Come on in!"

They stomped the snow from their feet and entered. "Dad," Corbin said with a smile and a spark in his eyes, "I'd like you to meet my girlfriend, Aimee Deveraux."

With a sharp intake of breath and a blink of surprise, she exclaimed, "That's the first time I've heard my new name aloud!" She laughed with delight. "I'm sorry, that must sound really crazy!" she said to his father.

"Corbin told me that you had just discovered your real parents. He said there was a lot more to it but that he would share it later, with your approval, of course." He smiled warmly. "Oh, and my name is Kenneth O'Malley," he said, holding out his hand cordially. "Corbin, you're right, she is very beautiful!"

"I know, right?" Corbin said, giving her a brief hug. "Do I see a present under the tree? For me I hope? Can I go and shake it?"

"You can open it, but let me make you my special hot buttered-rum drinks first, okay?" She quickly made their drinks from the simmering pot on the stove.

After they were all seated, Corbin opened his present. "I love it! I really needed a new case. My other one was a wreck. Thank you!" He blew her a kiss. Out of his pocket, he placed a small box in her hand. She opened it with shaky fingers.

A gold cross with a single diamond shone against the black velvet. "I love it! It's beautiful!"

He clasped it around her neck. "My Aimee." He breathed into her hair. "For hope and protection," he said, lightly kissing her. They sat comfortably, chatting about Christmas and past holidays that Corbin had shared with his father and brothers on their ranch in Bend, Oregon.

The lights flickered. Chewy's ears lifted. The Christmas music that had been playing lightly on the stereo ceased. Corbin slightly frowned, tilting his head. Corbin met her eyes. The room temperature began to drop. Chewy sat up at attention. A low growl emanated from his throat. The temperature dropped significantly more. Their breath appeared in the air in little clouds.

"No," Aimee mouthed silently.

Bewildered, Kenneth looked at both of them expectantly, waiting for an answer. The door to her office flung open and shut with a bang. They all jumped, and Chewy barked sharply. The lights went out. There was a distinctive sound coming from her office—a clackety sound. "What the hell is going on?" Kenneth demanded. The light from the fireplace illuminated his concerned face.

"Corbin, I don't understand…this should be over with now," she said with a quiet, hushed voice of agitation. The door to her office opened and slammed shut again.

Corbin stood up and took the flashlight off the mantel. "Dad, stay where you are. We'll explain everything in a bit."

He took her hand, and they began walking to her office with Chewy following close behind them. Chewy was growling and his hair was standing up on his haunches. Upon entering the room, the curtains billowed out furiously once and then settled back into place. Corbin shone the light on the typewriter. "Oh my God! There is something typed there! What in the world!"

She was gripping him tightly, her nails digging through his shirt. "Get closer! What does it say?" Her voice was stilted and hoarse. Her teeth chattered in the cold air.

He walked in closer, straining to see and with her closely clutching at his side. He reached over and pulled the paper from the typewriter. The air was so still, silent, and cold. His eyes were wide with surprise.

"Well, for the love of God, what does it say?" She had a deep sense of sudden foreboding.

He clenched the paper tightly in his hands. "It says I HAVE ANOTHER STORY!" They stared at each other in shock. A voice in the room began in a whisper. "Aimeeeeeee…sorrrrry…" The volume rose in intensity, chilling them to the bones with fear. "I HAVE ANOTHER STORY!"

The End